The
Streets
of Terror

BOOKS BY RUSS MORAN

THE TIME MAGNET NOVELS
The Gray Ship - Book 1
The Thanksgiving Gang - Book 2
Time of Fear - Book 3
The Skies of Time - Book 4
The Keepers of Time - Book 5

THE PATTERNS SERIES
The Shadows of Terror - Book 1
The Scent of Revenge - Book 2
A Reunion in Time – Book 3

THE MATT BLAKE MYSTERIES
Sideswiped - Book 1
The Reformers - Book 2
The President is Missing - Book 3
A Climate of Doubt - Book 4

THE HARRY AND MEG SERIES
The Maltese Incident – Book 1
The Violent Sea – Book 2
Sea of Fear – Book 3
The Pineaire Incident – Book 4

THE DETECTIVING SERIES
Until You Came Along – Book 1
The Streets of Terror – Book 2
Together We Win – Book 3
The Long Island Project – Book 4

THE WORMHOLE ADVENTURES
The Wormhole Gang – Book 1
The Wormhole Crisis – Book 2

Robot Depot

Leonardo Murphy

The Silent Author

A Charter Through Time

The Love We Almost Lost

The
Streets
of Terror

Book Two of the
Detectiving Series

Russell F. Moran

The Streets of Terror

Coddington Press

Copyright © 2019 by Russell F. Moran

Printed in the United States of America

ISBN-978-1-7377710-0-5

Covers and text design by LuAnn T. Palazzo.

www.morancom.com

DEDICATION

This book is dedicated to
America's police detectives.

FOREWORD

The Streets of Terror is a crime thriller and a love story, Book Two of the *Detectiving* series. It's about the adventures of detectives Bob Lawton and Bobbie Nelson. They're famous detectives and they love to uncover patterns—they love their profession, which they call *Detectiving*. They also love each other. Because of a nickname the Commissioner gave them, they are known as the famous BBs. They began their partnership with serious doubts about their relationship. That doubt soon disappeared as they started to respect each other's professional skills, and their deep affection for each other began to grow. Bob and Bobbie are two of my favorite characters, and I think of them as old friends. I imagine them sitting with me in a coffee shop as they tell me about their cases. As I wrote this book, we took a lot of adventures together. I hope you will see them that way too.

You will find a **Cast of Characters** after the last chapter of the book. It can be frustrating to come across a character on page 150, that you first met on page 20, especially if you've put the book down for a few days. I've seen this done in Russian literature, and I happily add a cast of characters to *The Streets of Terror* as well as my other novels.

The
Streets
of Terror

Book Two of the
Detectiving Series

Russell F. Moran

Coddington Press
Islip, NY

CHAPTER ONE

Bob Lawton

B ob, I have a confession to make, and if I don't I'll never get my life back."

"What is it?"

"I almost cheated on you."

I had just gotten back from a week-long seminar in California, and Bobbie's words hit my stomach like a sledgehammer.

"Define 'almost,'" I said.

"It's about that new detective the NYPD just hired, that sexy hunk, Ted Morris."

To hear my wife describe another man as "a sexy hunk" tore at my innards. I felt sad and angry at the same time.

"So, what about him, this *sexy hunk* as you describe him?"

"You were gone for only three days when he invited me to dinner. And I accepted."

"So, you went on a date with this guy, a date with a man who isn't your husband?"

She buried her face in my chest and, between sobs, filled me in on her "dinner date" with Mr. Hunk. She held back nothing, which we agree is what our marriage is all about, complete openness and honesty. She told me about her strong attraction to the guy, even filling me in on the details of her daydreaming and her thoughts of sex. She told me that Morris drove her to his house near the restaurant where they had their "date." It was, as Bobbie put it, the line of no return, the line of betrayal, the line of cheating—on me, her husband. She told me about her thoughts of screwing the guy, her lust for a casual tryst. As I said, Bobbie left nothing out. This wasn't easy to listen to—to hear that your wife had the hots for another man—and came close to acting on her feelings. Bobbie is a breathtakingly beautiful woman, a total knockout. It's easy to see why that guy hit on her, but it tore me apart that she actually considered reciprocating. But the only positive thing about this shock was that Bobbie was totally open with me—totally.

"I know you now hate me, Bob, and I don't blame you. I just had to tell you about my near betrayal of you, and if I didn't tell you everything, I'd take those thoughts to my grave. I hate myself. I'm so sorry, baby. Can you possibly forgive me?"

"So, if I understand you, you stopped short of having sex, is that true?"

"That's absolutely true!" Bobbie yelled. "At the last moment I managed to get my shit together and remember the man I married, the man I love. That would be you, baby. I suddenly remembered the word *commitment*, my commitment to you. The last thing I remember was telling him to go fuck himself. I hated him almost as much as I hated myself. And I definitely hated myself. I still do. Bob, please hold me, squeeze me. Please forgive me. Oh my God, do I love you. You're not just part of my life. You *are* my life."

I wrapped my arms around her. Love and warmth poured from her body. I knew it was torture for her to confess her innermost secrets.

It was also torture for me to hear her words about that "sexy hunk."

"What you just said, Bobbie, explains why I love you more than you can possibly imagine. You could have given me bullshit. You could have told me that it was all him with no feelings on your part. Actually, you didn't need to tell me anything at all. You could have kept all this stuff secret. But no, you value our love and honesty more than that. So, you found yourself attracted to him. Hell, he *is* a good-looking guy, and I can obviously understand why he was attracted to *you,* a woman of stunning beauty. And your attraction was only in your head. You refused to cross the line of no return, as you put it. The most important thing is that you *chose* to share all this with me. You just gave me total honesty, honey, in exchange for which I give you my total love."

We kissed as if it was our first time.

"Bob, I love you more than life itself. I mean shit, here I am telling you about my sleazy attraction to another man, and what is your reaction? Complete forgiveness and love. I cannot possibly live my life without you, baby."

And I can't live my life without her. In a strange way, Bobbie's confession about her thoughts on that piece of shit Lothario actually brought us closer together. She poured her heart out to me and held nothing back. If I ever doubted my love for Bobbie, tonight erased that doubt. She's my detective partner, my wife, and my lover. She's also my best friend.

So, our marriage had just been tested—as never before. But Bobbie's total honesty and our love for each other kept it together. I love this woman. How can I not?

———

Bobbie and I were partnered as First Grade Detectives two years ago. The NYPD was undergoing an agonizing period of scandal, both in the detective and uniformed ranks. Commissioner Norquist, on orders from Mayor Paxton, went on a mission to recruit the best detectives he could find from other police departments around the country. A prime focus of his search was Detective Bobbie Nelson of the Chicago Police Department. Probably the most famous detective in the country, Bobbie was widely known as the "Sherlock Holmes" of Chicago. He made her an excellent offer, the best his budget would allow for, and the NYPD hired her. She was assigned as my partner, as my then current partner was scheduled to retire. I was nervous as hell. Given her notoriety, I fully expected her to be an obnoxious scene-stealing bitch and that I'd be her boy-Friday.

Our first day together on the job changed my opinion drastically. Not only was she stunningly beautiful, but she had a polite, calm way about her that caused my heart to miss a beat. We were assigned to a huge multiple-murder case and drove there shortly after we met. It soon became apparent to me that not only was she gorgeous, she was one hell of a skilled detective. I had never seen a cop work a crime scene as professionally as she did. I was also impressed by her constant politeness toward me. When analyzing the facts in front of us, she would often reach out and touch my arm as if to let me know I was in on the deal. By the end of that first day, I had not only taken a liking to her, but I was also beginning to fall in love. Two months later we married. So, the woman I was prepared to hate had become my partner, my lover, my wife—and also my best friend. Bobbie is the real deal.

CHAPTER TWO

Bobbie

On Monday morning, Bob and I had breakfast at the diner, as usual. The diner is a short two block walk from our townhouse on Park Row, and two blocks away from our office at One Police Plaza, affectionately known as *One PP*. If we have one hardbound tradition in our lives, it's breakfast at the diner.

We both felt beyond relieved that I told Bob told me about my brief fling with that oversexed piece of shit, Ted Morris. We now feel closer to each other, if that's even possible. I couldn't let go of Bob's hand, not that I wanted to. There is something about complete honesty that enhances your love for somebody. And I was completely open and honest with Bob. If I didn't unload that shit from my chest, I'd take it to my grave. No surprise, he showed nothing but warmth and forgiveness. My God, do I love this man. My sexual attraction to that creep, Morris, was the first speed bump in our marriage, but at least I got it all on the table, all of it. Bob is my man and I'm his woman. That's it—all of it.

We had a pleasant surprise when Commissioner Norquist told us that he had fired Ted Morris. He said that he had received numerous credible reports that Morris viewed the women of the NYPD as "tasty items on a buffet table." I winced when he said that. "No fucking way will I allow the NYPD to put up with that shit," Commissioner

Ralph said in his normal blunt way. "That asshole is out of here." He also told us that the union president supported his decision to fire Mr. Loverboy.

When Commissioner Ralph told us that, we smiled at each other and held hands. A bad part of our lives was behind us, one that could have tested our marriage. With my total loving honesty, I prevented it from being a test. And Bob chimed in with his complete forgiveness. If anything, my dalliance with that piece of shit oddly brought us closer. Have I mentioned how much I love Bob?

———————

A few weeks later, we were in for a total shock. As we investigated a serial killer case, we discovered that the murderer was none other than my sexual pursuer, Ted Morris. I was stunned. Not only had I come close to betraying my wonderful husband, but I almost had sex with a serial killer, a man who murdered eight people. The case had been assigned to Bob and me, so we made the arrest once we had sufficient evidence. We collared him at a bar in Queens. We had found a coaster with the bar's name on it at one of the murder scenes. That was lover boy's big mistake. When he walked in, we both approached him with handcuffs. He jumped off the stool and attempted to run. Bob stopped him with a pile driver of a punch to his stomach. Former Marine Captain Bob throws a wicked punch. I've never been happier to collar someone. That creep, Morris, the lover boy killer, is now serving a life sentence, a life that doesn't include me.

Bob has a sometimes-nutty sense of humor, a tendency to crack dumb jokes. Shortly after we locked up Morris, Bob said to me: "You really need to work on your boyfriend-choosing skills."

I was furious, but Bob immediately apologized for his wisecrack. I buried my face in his big chest and hugged him. My God, do I love this man, dumb jokes and all.

We decided to celebrate by taking Ralph up on his offer for us head to our beach house in East Hampton. Bob and I recently co-authored a nonfiction book about what we do. *Detectiving* is the title and summarizes what the book is about. Given our backgrounds as detectives, we'd become quite famous, and we nailed a $15 Million advance from Random House. We celebrated with a beautiful waterfront vacation home.

Bob and I are working on a new book. Working? We really need to get something down on paper, although our live rehearsals are wonderful. The editorial staff at Random House loved our book, especially the title—*Detectiving*.

I will never forget the day we met with Tom and Mildred Cunningham, the editors from Random House, whom we first met by sheer coincidence on our honeymoon cruise. It was time to talk business.

"Since you folks were away," Tom Cunningham said, "I've been following you carefully in the papers, as well as doing some additional background research. That article about you in *The New York Times Magazine*, not to mention your appearance on *The Ellen Bellamy Show*, have made you guys police celebrities. Being awarded the Presidential Medal of Freedom has more than put you on the map. It also got the attention of senior management at Random House. Your book on detective work will become an instant classic. I've been authorized to offer you an advance of $10 million."

"Fifteen," I said without batting an eye. After what Bob and I have been through I'd developed a few extra pounds of mojo.

"How about 12?" he said.

"Fifteen is better, much better," I said.

He reached his hand across the desk. "Deal."

He then handed us a contract, with the understanding that we would pass it by our lawyer.

So, we're on our way to becoming big-time authors. *Detectiving*, the weirdest-named book ever, would soon be launched. I felt confident we'd get the job done. I love to write and so does Bob, a best-selling author himself. We were happy as pigs in mud with our book deal. I think our banker will be happy too. I wondered what would await us at One PP when we return to our office next week.

We'd soon discover that our forthcoming book wasn't the only major item on our agenda.

Not even close.

CHAPTER THREE

Bob

Our meeting at Random House lasted three hours, although the contract negotiation took only 10 minutes, thanks to my wife's well-honed chutzpah. As sweet and gentle as she is, Bobbie knows how to drive a hard bargain. Wow, $15 Million. And that's only the advance.

Bobbie and I don't like to waste time, and when we latch onto something new, we like to get it done. Hey, we fell in love with each other in a month. We wanted to get a solid jump on our latest project, the forthcoming book, *Detectiving*, by Bobbie Nelson and Bob Lawton. So, we took another week off and got to work, treating the book project as a case.

I love writing fiction, and I managed to get it right with my best-selling novel, *An Army of Blue*. When I write fiction, I don't do a detailed outline, because I find it impossible to envision an entire story from beginning to end. When I began my novel, I tried to do a formal outline after reading a book on that subject. I tried and tried, but it just didn't work. Stories have a way of unfolding in front of you, which is why it's so much fun writing fiction. You surprise yourself, or rather the story surprises you. My novel kept taking off in interesting new directions, and each time it did I would need to revise the goddam outline. I finally packed it in and decided to heed the advice of the great Stephen King—Come up with a general idea of the story, then populate the pages with interesting characters, and let the characters show you how the story unfolds. So, I did just that and I had a blast. I became a "panster," a writer who flies by the seat of his pants. I also managed to sell a piss-load of books.

Non-fiction is different, as both Bobbie and I agreed, and so did Mildred Cunningham, our editor at Random House. We needed a detailed outline first and would then write the book. Not to brag, but Bobbie and I know a hell of a lot about the business of being detectives. That's what landed us the book deal in the first place. So, we began our careful outline.

Bobbie came up with the idea that parts of the book should read like a novel, although we would keep to the facts strictly as if it were a newspaper article. So, I began to come up with chapters about cases we both had worked on, either together or before we met. The only factual difference would be fictional names, except for names of those who were actually convicted, which was public knowledge anyway.

Our outline poured out smoothly. Here is the first outline draft of *Detectiving:*

Chapter 1 – Overview of Law Enforcement in the United States

Chapter 2 – The Differences Between Uniformed Police Officers and Detectives

Chapter 3 – The Education of Law Enforcement Officers

Chapter 4 – The Equipment Used, Including Firearms

Chapter 5 – Arrest Procedures

Chapter 6 – Search Procedures

Chapter 7 – Crime Scene Investigations

Chapter 8 – Blood Analysis, Including Different Types of Stains

Subchapter – Everything you Ever Need to Know About Flies and Other Insects

Subchapter – Scientific and Mathematical issues

Chapter 9 – Fingerprints

Chapter 10 – DNA Analysis

Chapter 11 – The Fine Art of Interrogating a Witness

Chapter 12 – The Legal Process and the Courts

Chapter 13 – Punishment—Jails, Prisons, and the Death Penalty

Interspersed within and between these chapters would be our "war stories," written in fiction-style by me.

By the end of the day, Bobbie and I realized we had our basic outline. It only took us a day and a half. We know our stuff.

As we worked, we would brainstorm on what we call "beats," ideas and scenes that we want to include. After that, we would fit the beats into the appropriate chapters.

At 6 p.m. on Wednesday, Bobbie suggested we relax and that I mix us some martinis while she took a quick shower. She walked back into the room, barefoot, wearing a gorgeous short negligee that wrapped around her stunning body like a caress. We were about to write a very exciting chapter.

CHAPTER FOUR

Bob

Commissioner Norquist, or Ralph as we address him now, called Bobbie and me into his office.

"You two have been working your asses off and I want you to take a few days off. Go and enjoy your beach house in East Hampton. I've said it so many times, I'm almost tired of listening to myself, but you two are the best detectives in the NYPD. In the meantime, enjoy the salt air. So, my friends, head east and chill for a few days. You BBs have earned it."

Ralph had nicknamed us "the BBs," and Bobbie and I love it. It tells the world the truth—that we're one entity.

"Ralph," Bobbie said, "I can't believe this. The only reason for this meeting is to give us some time off?"

"Of course not," he said laughing as he handed Bobbie a file. "Here's a triple homicide I want you to work on. You BBs love to keep busy. It will give you something to do when you're not smelling the ocean air and walking along the beach. See you guys next week."

After we walked into our sparkling beach house in East Hampton and unpacked, Bobbie and I decided to go antique store browsing in the village. The weather was perfect, and we enjoyed our walk. We even left our guns in a locker back at the house. We bought a couple of antiques we thought would look great in our Manhattan apartment. We were, to use a word strange to us, relaxing. But, typical of Bobbie and me, we came up with an exciting new writing project, a sequel to *Detectiving*.

CHAPTER FIVE

Bobbie

After our walk through the village, we both felt a bit sweaty, which made me happy as hell. "Sweaty" meant it was time for a shower, and a shower meant sex with my gorgeous husband. The shower room came equipped with a waterproof couch, which provided multiple ways of experimenting with different positions. We even keep a written list of codenames for our changing positions. One of my favorites is "climbing the mountain," which means, well, don't ask. We may be nuts, but we're happily-in-love nuts.

After our sexy shower, we dried off, got into jeans and sweatshirts, and dug into the planning for our next book, the sequel to *Detectiving*, a history of famous detectives, both real and fictional, but mainly fictional. But even the fictional characters were based on real people. We didn't limit ourselves to research on books, but included movies and TV shows. We came up with a list of 25 major detective characters, which we would start with and add to later. We decided to go with a list of detectives in order of popularity.

Number one was no surprise, ***Sherlock Holmes***, the memorable character created by Arthur Conan Doyle. Sherlock Holmes has been portrayed in countless movies and TV dramas as an incredibly intuitive character. Holmes said the famous words to his sidekick Dr.

Watson, "It's elementary dear Watson." Needless to say, I got a big kick out of the *Chicago Tribune* referring to me, Bobbie Nelson, as a "real life Sherlock Holmes." Although those words were written tongue-in-cheek, I couldn't have been more honored.

Second on the list was none other than **Lieutenant Columbo**, memorably portrayed on the TV series by the late actor Peter Falk. Columbo was a frumpily dressed, cigar-chomping, mess of a man. He always wore his famous wrinkled tan raincoat. He's famous for the words, "Somethin's bodderin me," and "Just one more thing." And one more thing means that Detective Columbo had solved the case.

Next came Detective **Jessica Fletcher**, portrayed on the popular TV series, "Murder She Wrote," by the acclaimed actress Angela Lansbury. Detective Fletcher was bothered by all the unsolved murders in Cabot Cove, Maine, and then, week after week, solved them all between commercials. Lansbury was not a detective by training but an inquisitive novelist.

Teenage **Nancy Drew** is the opposite in age from Jessica Fletcher. Although an untrained kid, she has an uncanny ability to solve puzzles. She was created by Edward Stratenmeyer. The Nancy Drew stories began in 1930 as the *Nancy Drew Mystery Series,* and have been written by a number of ghost writers under the pen name Carolyn Keene. *The Girl Detective Series* began in 2004, and was replaced in 2013 as *The Nancy Drew Diaries*. Nancy Drew has attracted young-adult readers and film goers for decades.

The Hardy Boys, starring Joe and Frank Hardy, is another young-adult favorite and has been the subject of dozens of novels. The boys get their cases from a secret group known as ATAC, *American Teens against Crime*. The long-running *Hardy Boys Mystery Stories* ended in 2005 and was replaced by a rebooted series. The Hardy Boys were introduced in 1927, and have gone through extensive changes over the years.

Philip Marlow, created by Raymond Chandler, was a hard-boiled Los Angeles detective, although in private he was philosophical and loved chess and poetry. He was played over the years by major actors like Humphrey Bogart, Robert Mitchum, Elliott Gould, and James Garner. He first appeared under that name in *The Big Sleep* in 1939. He also appeared as a similar character with names like "Carmady" and "John Dalmas."

───────

After we completed our writing chores in the den, Bobbie sat down at the kitchen counter while I made us a shaker of martinis. We looked at each other and both had the same thought. We've gotten to know each other's thinking just from a glance. We may be enjoying some seaside relaxation, but we both had the same thought—It's time to get to work. So, I picked up our new multiple murder file, set it on the counter, and opened it. I read aloud from the summary on the first page.

We then went page by page, making careful notes as we always do. The case was about a triple homicide of a family from the Riverdale section of the Bronx. A 35-year-old mother, her 13-year-old daughter, and 15-year-old son had been killed, each shot in the head.

A Department of Justice study disclosed that 62% of violent crimes were committed by offenders known to the victims. As any detective will tell you, the perpetrator is often a close family member, sometimes even the father.

But in this case, the father had died of a heart attack two years before. The two detectives assigned to the case before us, (who knew that the case would eventually be assigned to Bobbie and me) had done some excellent preliminary investigation, including poring over emails from the mother and the two kids. Nothing disclosed any ill will between the victims and anyone with whom they corresponded.

The detectives fanned out and interrogated neighbor after neighbor, as they should. Nothing. There was no evidence of shouting, or that the family had troubles with anybody. Every neighbor they spoke to expressed shock that such nice people were murdered. The CSU unit gathered all the necessary blood evidence and fingerprints. None of the prints matched any criminal or suspect in the NYPD files. It could have been a random killing.

Although I would never say it to anyone but Bobbie, it soon became apparent why Commissioner Ralph wanted us to handle the case. It was a puzzle, and nobody figures out puzzles better than Bobbie and me. This would be a tough case, just the kind we like to work on. It will require every bit of *Detectiving*, something that Bobbie and I love.

I poured our martinis and sat next to Bobbie. We clinked glasses and kissed.

"So, partner, how do you think we should proceed?"

She smiled and stroked my face.

"Like we always do—*together*."

CHAPTER SIX

Bobbie

W ow, you look pretty this morning," Bob said.

"Don't tell me I look pretty when I'm pissed off."

"Okay, you look pretty pissed off."

I cracked up. Leave it to Bob derail my self-centered anger with his wise-ass humor.

"What's the matter, baby?" Bob said.

"I'm a friggin First Grade detective and I shouldn't have to put up with shit from a clerk in the records office."

I had inadvertently placed my working file folder under a folder that contained evidence from a crime scene. Simple mistake, which should have been simply corrected by the clerk. But no, she wanted a written order from Commissioner Norquist, who happened to be out of town for five days. And now I'm without my file folder, which includes my notebook. I can do without my notebook as easily as I can do without my eyes.

Bob volunteered to handle the problem, of course. My partner is insanely handsome, and all the clerks in the records office are women. Bob returned five minutes later. He didn't just convince the clerk to surrender the folder—she actually handed it to Bob.

"Thanks, honey," I said. "You sure have a convincing way with women, don't you?"

"Well, I convinced you to marry me, didn't I?"

Bob and I had just returned from our relaxing week in East Hampton. We spent most of the time in bed, or in the pool, or on the beach—making love. There's something about salt air and sex that go together perfectly.

As usual, we used some of our vacation time to work a file, a difficult file—*The Morton Case,* a triple murder of a young woman and her two teenagers.

Loretta Morton, age 35, was found in the kitchen, dead of a gunshot wound to her head. Her daughter, Janice Morton, age 13, along with her 15-year-old brother Jason, were found in the living room, also dead from gunshots to the head. The detectives who did the initial case workup while Bob and I were away did a good job, but their thorough work didn't come up with a clue—not one goddam clue. This was shaping up to be the kind of case that Bob and I love to work—a tough case, even though a sad one.

Although the Bronx isn't known for beauty, the Riverdale area is a pretty, almost suburban neighborhood of expensive homes and condos. The Morton house was large and was situated on a half-acre overlooking the Hudson River. When Bob and I visited the place, I immediately noticed that the property was surrounded by tall hedges. That may provide privacy, but it it also gives cover to prowlers—or assassins. The late Thomas Morton was a wealthy art dealer and left his family well-provided for. One fortunate thing for our investigation was that Thomas Morton was quite well-known and showed up in the newspapers and magazines often. Loretta Morton was also somewhat famous as a talented ceramic artist. Our first task was to find what may be hiding in plain sight—on the Internet.

So as not to duplicate our efforts, Bob and I agreed that I would concentrate on researching Thomas Morton, and Bob would research the murder victims, Loretta Morton and the two kids, Janice and Franklin.

Bob and I love to work together, but sometimes our work is tedious, such as poring through the Internet looking for data points that intersect, especially data points involving names. Whenever we came across a name in the same article as one of our target names, we would tell each other, and then we'd make a note of that name in our separate files.

I was glad we faced each other across the desk. Whenever I felt angst coming on, I would take a moment to stare into Bob's hazel eyes, which always calmed me. You would think I'd get used those gorgeous eyes. Never happened, and I don't think it ever will, not that I want it to.

After hammering away for three hours, we noticed a name that appeared often, and in articles about each of our targets, Thomas, Loretta, Janice, and Franklin Morton. The name was Angelo DiCrispino. Nothing dramatic, nothing that could be called a clue— except the constant appearance of his name was a clue in itself.

Bob said he'd temporarily stop searching for the three family members and would concentrate on Angelo DiCrispino. I readily agreed. Who is this guy, and why does his name keep appearing near our target names?

CHAPTER SEVEN

Bob

Angelo DiCrispino isn't a unique name, but it's not a common one, like John Smith. I found a lot of Angelo DiCrispinos in my Internet search, most of whom showed nothing remarkable, except for one. An Angelo DiCrispino is a mob enforcer from New York City, a Mafia hit man in other words. A number of newspaper articles, as well as NYPD records, made his mob involvement apparent. Hold on, slow down. Just because I found a guy with the name of a known criminal doesn't mean it has anything to do with our case, as my outside-the-box-thinking partner reminded me. But it *is* a piece of information I need to chase down. Could these murders have been organized crime hits? Something worth speculating about.

I bounced my ideas off Bobbie, as she does with me. We love to put our minds together, not only our bodies. Bobbie agreed that Angelo DiCrispino deserves attention, a lot of attention.

CHAPTER EIGHT

Bobbie

Bob and I found numerous mentions of a guy named Angelo DiCrispino in the same articles as our murder victims as well as the late father who died of a heart attack. But *did* he die of a heart attack? My ever-diligent Bob went to the hospital and looked up the autopsy report. An NYPD shield gives you access to information that would normally be considered confidential. Yes, it was a heart attack, but there was more. The report read, "Cardiac arrest secondary to a choking incident." The summary cause of death was 'homicide,' followed by a question mark. I hate it when a medical examiner inserts a question mark. But even though I hated it, there's nothing I can do about it. Could the father, Thomas Morton, have been murdered as well as the mother and two kids?

Bob tracked down everything he could find on the mysterious Angelo DiCrispino, and we discovered that a man by that name is a mob enforcer, a hit man.

"He once lived in Chicago," Bob said, "and he worked with the local Mafia, which had been almost obliterated in 1943 when they nailed the crime legend, Al Capone. The man now lives in New York, in Riverdale. Interesting—he lives in Riverdale, where the Mortons once lived and were murdered."

Because of DiCrispino's numerous scrapes with law enforcement, his fingerprints and DNA were on file. So, it's simply a matter of comparing the prints and DNA, which the original detectives found when they inspected the crime scene. Simple, no? But no print or DNA sample matched that of DiCrispino, not one. We were disappointed, but not surprised. Hit men, who kill for a living, are experts in hiding their tracks. Bob and I would soon learn that DiCrispino's employer has been on the rise. The mob was no longer defeated.

CHAPTER NINE

Bob

Bobbie and I walked to our favorite diner for our usual breakfast. I got it right a few years ago when I bought a condo, a whole building actually, such a short walk from where I work. I now share it with Bobbie, my wife, my partner, my lover. Because it's so close to the office, we often take an extended lunch hour so we can, well, why not?

As we walked into the diner, hand in hand, we were greeted by a few of our fellow cops. Everybody seems to know that Bobbie and I are crazy about each other. They also respect our professionalism. I must admit that we're damn good detectives, especially Bobbie. I've always been proud of my work, but there was something refreshing about being a student of my partner, yes, a student. Bobbie knows her stuff. She's the smartest cop I've ever met, not to mention the foxiest.

After breakfast we walked to One PP, arriving at 8:15 a.m. We like to get to work early. After we walked into our office and closed the door, we hugged and kissed. It may seem crazy for two married people, who made passionate love the night before, to begin their day at the office with a hug and a kiss. But that's the way it is with Bobbie and me. It's what we do. It's who we are. And I intend to keep it that way. Bobbie always keeps a small bottle of hand wash in her purse to wipe the lipstick off my face.

Margie Nathan, Commissioner Ralph's assistant, knocked and entered our office with a huge file under her arm.

"Here's more stuff on the *Palermo Incident Case,*" Margie said. "The Commissioner called me this morning, even though he's on vacation, and told me to give this new material to you. He asks that you give this case your undivided attention, not that I need to tell that to you guys. Enjoy, BBs, you have some big work cut out for you." As Ralph's assistant said, Bobbie and I have our work cut out for us. And, because Bobbie and I are now on the case, so does the mob. I'm half Italian, as is Bobbie, and it sickened us to see these creeps besmirching our proud heritage. From what I've read, Rudy Giuliani was also motivated by his Italian legacy.

Everybody seems to call us the BBs, and I'm getting to love it. Bobbie and Bob—*the BBs*. It announces to the world the truth, that Bobbie and I are one and the same.

Before he left for vacation, Norquist dropped a bomb on us, a matter we call *The Palermo Incident* case. It seems that the mob, aka the Mafia, aka *La Cosa Nostra*, is in resurgence, a huge resurgence. Ever since the Giuliani administration, everybody thought the Mafia was old history, the stuff of movies and TV dramas. Not so, or I should say, no longer so.

In the Mafia Commission Trial, which ran from February 1985 through November 1986, then U.S. Attorney Giuliani indicted 11 organized crime figures, including the heads of New York's infamous "Five Families," under the Racketeer Influenced and Corrupt Organizations Act (RICO). The charges included extortion, labor racketeering, and murder for hire. *Time* magazine called this the "Case of Cases," possibly "the most significant assault on organized crime since the high command of the Chicago Mafia was swept away in 1943." The *Times* quoted Giuliani's stated intention:

"Our approach is to wipe out the five families."

Gambino crime family boss Paul Castellano evaded conviction when he and his underboss, Thomas Bilotti, were murdered on the streets of Midtown Manhattan in December, 1985.

Three other heads of the Five Families were sentenced to 100 years in prison in January 1987. The Genovese and Colombo family leaders, Tony Salerno and Carmine Persico, received additional sentences in separate trials, with 70-year and 39-year sentences to run consecutively.

Most observers believed that Giuliani rid the country of some of the worst criminals at large. Or so it seemed. But it didn't last, as recent events have been telling us.

The Five Families still exist, although with new names. They are now the Marquessa, Gandolfo, Rubino, Lombardo, and Critello families. And they've expanded their portfolio of activities from extortion, labor racketeering, and murder for hire. Although they're still involved with those lovely enterprises, they now include massive drug smuggling, prostitution, and online gambling. As Ralph's assistant said, Bobbie and I have our work cut out for us. And, because Bobbie and I are now on the case, so does the mob. I'm half Italian, as is Bobbie, and it sickened us to see these creeps besmirching our proud heritage. From what I've read, Rudy Giuliani was motivated by his Italian legacy.

Because the two of us have strong suspicions about the mob hit man, Angelo DiCrispino, we included the Morton murders with our Mafia cases, especially the *Palermo Incident* case.

The Mafia Commission Trial in the 1980s was an FBI operation. But now, on specific orders from the attorney general, Bobbie and I would lead the new investigation. We've become kind of famous recently, having busted a couple of large cases. Bobbie was already a police celebrity from her days as the "Sherlock Holmes of the

Chicago Police Department." We were enjoying our day in the sun. Commissioner Norquist, or Ralph as we now call him, is a friend as well as a boss. He kindly, if somewhat embarrassingly, refers to us as "NYPD *royalty*."

Well, royalty or not, we have work to do. TV police dramas often portray detectives as swashbuckling gunslingers, who violently defeat the bad guys each week between commercials. The reality is that detective work means interrogating witnesses, examining blood stains, analyzing fingerprints, and hours of looking at evidence. Yes, we carry guns, but unlike the cops on TV, we seldom use them. The only times I've fired my gun, not counting my time as a Marine Captain in Iraq, was on the practice shooting range. Bobbie only fired her weapon once in the line of duty, when she saved my life by killing a would-be assassin.

I married well.

"Honey, this is a big one," Bobbie said.

"Big one? I'd say so. Two American senators and a congressman have been assassinated in Sicily. The commissioner is calling this the *Palermo Incident* case. The CIA will have jurisdiction over there, but we can at least start digging. Let's review what we know already. Your thoughts?"

"We know that both senators and the congressman were investigating the Mafia, and were very public about it," Bobbie said. "I recall when Rudy Giuliani headed up that mob trial in the 80s when he was U.S. Attorney for the Southern District of New York, the Sicilian Mafia offered $800,000 for his hide. These bastards play for keeps, Bob. The FBI investigations, as well as our own, tell us that the mob is playing a new role, a *big* new role. They've squeezed out the low-level loan sharks and other turds and are now bringing it all in under the Mafia brand. We need to be careful, Bob. I don't think we should go anywhere without protection, and I don't mean just our own guns.

Shit, if they're willing to whack elected government officials, you and I are small fry. Thank God Ralph has assigned us bodyguards."

Bobbie and I were concerned that we may be on the hit list.

We'd soon find out that our concerns were well-founded.

CHAPTER TEN

Bob

At 6:30 p.m., we walked to our apartment. As I followed her through the door, Bobbie screamed, "Bob, stop!" She lowered her shoulder and pushed me back into the hallway, like a running back throwing a block. The force of the explosion blew the door open. It hung there, cockeyed, on its hinges. We hugged, wrapped in the sickening feeling that we had just missed being killed. Bobbie would later tell me that, as soon as we walked into the apartment, she saw a package on the floor next to the kitchen counter. If you see something, say something, or in Bobbie's case, *do something*. Once again, she saved my life—and hers. I'm blessed with a great partner, a beautiful, petite woman who knows how to throw a block.

Our bodyguards weren't injured because they walked behind us.

Our apartment became a crime scene for the next 24 hours. The kitchen and den were totally destroyed, and the rest of the place smelled of bomb smoke. The clothing in our drawers and closets was covered in the smoke, so we told our driver to take us to a nearby store where we would pick up new duds. Our bodyguards accompanied us. For the near future our new home would be the nearby *Marriott Residence Inn*.

How the hell do we get any investigating done from a hotel room? But then the thought occurred to me that we couldn't get anything done if we were dead.

CHAPTER ELEVEN

Bobbie

Bob and I sat in the den of our *Marriott Residence* unit. We were under strict orders not to move, orders straight from Commissioner Ralph, even though he was on vacation.

At 8:30 a.m. the phone rang. It was the Commissioner. "I'll be there in 10 minutes," he said.

"But you're supposed to be taking a well-earned vacation," I said, but he had already hung up.

The doorbell rang and Ralph Norquist walked in, accompanied by one of our bodyguards.

"Vacation or not," Ralph said, "when my two best detectives, not to mention my good friends, almost got fucking killed, I knew I had to come here. You two are going to hate what I'm about to say, but I'm putting you into the Witness Protection Program, and I've already cleared it with the FBI. The place where you'll be staying isn't far from here, and you'll be closely guarded. The Mafia plays rough, as you saw last night when you were almost killed by a bomb. No fucking way will I give them another chance."

Ralph finds it difficult to utter a few sentences without using the word "fucking."

"But Ralph, how can Bob and I interrogate people from behind closed doors?"

"For the time being, and I have no idea how long that may be, you will be out of the interrogation business, even though you and Bob are the best on the block when it comes to questioning witnesses. But you can't question people if you're dead. As you will see shortly, the place where you'll be taken is large and comfortable. You two will spend your time reviewing files and analyzing forensic evidence. I'm sorry, but this isn't negotiable. I want you two alive, my friends."

An hour later we were taken to a beautiful brownstone on East 65th Street. We underwent a *do-over* by a police makeup artist. Bob was given blond wig and a beard and wore a pillow under his shirt to make him look heavy. My blond hair was covered in a black wig, and I was also plumped up with stuffing under my clothes. We both wore dark-rimmed eyeglasses.

"Hey, chubby lady, you look alluring," Bob said.

"You too, fatso. C'mon let's get undisguised."

After we changed into normal clothes, we toured our new surroundings. Just as Ralph Norquist said, the place was beautiful. Two floors of our own, and an apartment downstairs for our bodyguards. It had a huge den, with a plexiglass-surrounded terrace that had a great view of Central Park. It sported three bedrooms, two and a half bathrooms, a well-equipped gym, an eat-in kitchen, and a small dining room. Bob and I agreed that it was the prettiest prison we could imagine. But it *was* a prison.

Above us was a lovely rooftop garden with a running track surrounding it. A small table created an outdoor eating area for enjoying meals outside in good weather. The windows, of course, were all bullet-proof plexiglass. Witness Protection means *witness protection.*

As Bob was inspecting the gym, I decided to rummage through a large steamer trunk in the corner of the den. I couldn't believe my eyes. "Oh, my God," I yelled. "Look, Bob, our favorite boardgame, *Clue.* There was also a chess set, checkers, multiple decks of cards, *Monopoly,* and *Risk.*

We both knew we'd be busy analyzing evidence, but it can only go so far without people to interrogate, and we had none. We'd have plenty of time for games, working on our book, as well as the usual playing around that Bob and I love. We may be prisoners against our will, but it was beginning to look like fun. We had a light dinner—the fridge was amply stocked with food—and played a game of *Clue.* It was almost a draw, but I won.

We still had some work to do on the project for which we had been paid a $15 million advance—*Detectiving,* our soon-to-be-launched book.

When we spent a week at the beach house, we got a ton of work done on the book. Bob and I submitted the first draft to our editor, Mildred Cunningham from Random House. After we worked on Mildred's edits for a couple of hours, we were both tired, but I wanted to put some positive thoughts in our heads before we went to bed, something to give us perspective on being in the Witness Protection Program.

"Hey, Bob," I said. "Let's think about some things we should be happy about. You go first."

"We're alive," Bob said.

"We're uninjured," I said.

"We're in love," we both said.

CHAPTER TWELVE

Bob

B obbie and I were beginning to hate the Witness Protection
Program. We'd been locked up in this apartment for two
goddam months. We're both accustomed to getting things
done, to making things happen. Hey, we're cops, we're detectives.
We both love our work, because of what we do—*Detectiving*. But
being locked up doesn't make it easy to solve anything, even though
the surroundings are beautiful.

Yes, we play games a lot. Bobbie, with her devilish imagination,
even came up with the idea to play strip poker. But we're not cut
out to play games, although I must admit the strip poker is exciting,
especially because I'm a good poker player. I love baring her
gorgeous body, one article of clothing at a time.

Our editor was happy with the draft we sent her, but of course,
as a good editor, she had excellent suggestions and demands. So far,
we'd hit all the deadlines she set for us, and we expected to finish the
rewrite in three weeks. But we both felt restless.

The mob investigation team, of which Bobbie and I are
supposedly in charge, has been busy gathering information, but
information gathering can only go so far without hitting the streets
and asking questions. Commissioner Ralph wants to keep us safe,

and I can't disagree with him. Hell, after our apartment was bombed, we realized that we're targets. But Bobbie and I have always taken our work seriously, and it's hard to be serious when locked up in an apartment. At least we make love a lot—a lot—but then we always do, without being imprisoned.

Bobbie's going stir crazy too.

CHAPTER THIRTEEN

Bobbie

Being a prisoner is no fun, even when you're in beautiful surroundings. It does have certain benefits. Our sex life has always been best described as "frisky," but here, we make love at least once a day, sometimes twice. Hell, yesterday we did it three times. Nothing like an exciting game of strip poker to get your juices flowing. Bob's just plain sweet, and never stops surprising me. I don't just love him, I *like* him. We're spouses, we're partners, we're lovers, but we're also best friends.

But we both agreed that the Witness Protection Program was getting on our nerves. Bob and I have handled some huge cases, solving puzzles like we always do. We wrapped up that big terrorist plot where cops around the country were being assassinated. Then we cracked the case involving the horrible gang, MS-13, where they were harvesting body organs from innocent young people.

But we're anxious to get back to our work. Some have called us the two best detectives on the street, and we want to resume doing what we do so well—*Detectiving*. Working with Bob is great. Good partners know how to bounce ideas off each other, and we do just that. Bob has a finely-honed sense of logic. He would put together pieces of evidence that took us toward a solution. I'm more intuitive, on the other hand. Bob tells me that I think outside the box, and that's true. As he loves to say, I walk East when others walk West. So, we complement each other perfectly. Being in love with your partner is a bonus, a wonderful bonus.

But Bob and I need to get back to doing what we're good at, and I don't mean passionate sex, although we love to do just that. We need to find patterns.

What we didn't know is that tomorrow we'd have an answer to our restlessness in the Witness Protection Program.

CHAPTER FOURTEEN

Bob

At 2 p.m. one of our bodyguards buzzed us and said we had a visitor, and that it had been cleared with headquarters. When I asked him who it was, he said we'd find out soon enough. Why the cloak and dagger?

Our doorbell rang and when I opened it, there was none other than Sarah Watson, Director of the FBI.

Bobbie and I had met her many times before. She's one of our favorite people—pretty, soft-spoken, polite, and a sweetheart of a human being. She's also tough as nails and talented at what she does, which is running the most important law enforcement agency in the country.

"Bobbie and Bob, it's great to see you two again. You've done great work for the NYPD, the FBI, the CIA, and not to mention the nation. As I've said many times before, you two are the best detectives in the country."

Uh-oh. Could there be an agenda behind all this flattery?

"So how do you like it in the Witness Protection Program?" she asked.

"It sucks. To be honest, Sarah, Bobbie and I don't feel like we're getting anything done."

"I think I may have a solution for that," she said. "As you're well aware, the country's problem with organized crime has recently hit crisis proportions. Hell, that's why you folks are here, because of a mob assassination attempt on you. It's gotten bad and is getting worse as we speak. *The Palermo Incident*, as it's called, where two Senators and a Congressman were killed, has law enforcement in crisis mode, especially the FBI. I have agents fanned out across the country trying to get a handle on all this. We're working closely with the CIA, which has a small army of agents in Palermo."

"So, is this a Sicilian problem?" Bobbie asked.

"That would make it a bit easier, at least from an intelligence gathering point of view. Yes, it is a Sicilian problem, but it's also an American problem. The Sicilian Mafia has morphed into hundreds of smaller units, and the foot soldiers aren't just Sicilian. History tells us that the Mafia in Chicago was wiped out during World War II in 1943. After that came the successful efforts by Rudy Giuliani in taking down the infamous Five Families in New York. What were once the Bonanno, Colombo, Gambino, Genovese, and Lucchese families, have been replaced by the Marquessa, Gandolfo, Rubino, Lombardo, and Critello families. I'm sure you two are aware of this because I know you like to keep on top of things. But these aren't just name changes. The mob units have strengthened, grown, and are heavily financed. To put it bluntly, the Five Families are back. And here's something that may shock you. The old Chicago Mafia that died in 1943 when Al Capone went to prison, has also made a resurgence, a huge resurgence. The City of Chicago has always had a serious problem with corruption, as you well know Bobbie, having lived and worked there for many years."

Bobbie raised her eyebrows as if to say, "Tell me about it."

"Let me guess," Bobbie said, "the government of Chicago is in bed with the mob."

"You got that right, Bobbie. Just like in the days of Al Capone, you can't tell where the mob stops and the government starts."

"Is there a lot of cooperation among the Mafia families?" I asked.

"More than cooperation, Bob. The American Mafia, if I can use such a term, has become corporate and sophisticated. It's no longer the days of a guy jumping out of a car with a machine gun, although that still happens. The mob has been studying the way big successful corporations run, and they're patterning themselves that way. The big difference, of course, is the end product of its activities—murder, mayhem, and all sorts of criminal shit. We're seeing a gigantic enterprise of loan sharking, murder for hire, drugs, and prostitution, just to name a few of its product lines. Where good companies fear to tread, the mob happily fills the shelves."

Somehow all this involves Bobbie and me, otherwise she wouldn't be here. I figured I'd get right to the point.

"How does all this involve Bobbie and me, Sarah?"

"I'm dusting off your status as provisional FBI agents and I'm reappointing you. You won't go through an update of your background check because we want to keep this secret, and having a bunch of people asking questions about you could also raise some questions with the mob, which listens closely. You folks haven't been involved in any illegal activities the FBI should know about, I assume," she said with a laugh.

"Bob cheats at strip poker," Bobbie said.

Sarah cracked up. "I'll make careful note of that for the record."

"All of which brings me to the reason for our meeting. Bobbie and Bob, I'm requesting that you two go undercover—deep undercover— and that you move temporarily to Chicago, the new center of the Mafia's activities. You will live in Evanston, a pretty suburb on the northern border of Chicago. I say that I'm requesting it because I refuse to order you to do this because it may be dangerous. A good makeup artist can work wonders, as you found when you moved here to the WPP. I recommend that you immediately start to grow a real beard, Bob. Bobbie, you're probably the prettiest detective on the street, but we can change that."

"Oh, great, Detective Skank reporting for duty," Bobbie said.

"Don't worry, Bobbie, you'll still be pretty as Bob will be happy to know, but you'll be different, quite different, whenever you leave your house. Pads under clothing can make a big difference. And you can remove them at night—when Bob cheats at strip poker," she said with a laugh.

"Can Bobbie and I talk this over and let you know tomorrow?"

"Of, course; take longer if you wish. If you accept, you will live in a lovely, secure place and will have four bodyguards with you at all times. We'll talk again soon."

When Sarah left, Bobbie and I sat on the couch.

"So, what do you think, honey?" Bobbie said. "Do you want to go back into the spy business?"

"First I have a question. Who said I cheat at strip poker?"

"I was only kidding. I *let* you win. Hey, let's grab a deck of cards and talk about the FBI stuff later."

CHAPTER FIFTEEN

Bobbie

We woke up to a beautiful late April morning and decided to have a light breakfast on our rooftop garden. We had a big decision to make after our visit from Sarah Watson.

"So, what do you think, Bob, should we take up Sarah on her clandestine operation and move to Chicago?"

"I like the idea, but only if you do, honey. You lived in Chicago for a long time, so we won't feel lost. You sure as hell know your way around the city, so we should be able to get the job done."

"Like we always do?" I said.

"Yeah, like we always do, partner. I'm not too crazy about getting padded up like a freak every day, but it will be a nice break after being cooped up here. And we'll still be in the most important place—*together*."

"I say let's do it, honey," I said. "Like you, I'm fed up with this Witness Protection Program. Hell, we'll have four bodyguards and we'll be disguised, so the danger should be minimal. Sarah said she'd break the news to Ralph Norquist if we agree. I think this will be exciting."

CHAPTER SIXTEEN

Bob

In two weeks, we were ready to move to Chicago. Our flight was scheduled for later in the afternoon.

At 8 a.m. our makeup artists arrived. My beard was starting to grow in after two weeks, so I didn't need to worry about glue all over my face. We insisted that we each be made up separately in other rooms because we wanted to see how we looked at first glance. I was now a blond, with a blond beard to match. An FBI makeup artist would visit us every two weeks in Chicago to keep our new hair color in shape. Our padding wasn't designed to make us look obese, just overweight.

The time had come, and we both walked into the den.

Bobbie, my gorgeous shapely blond Bobbie, was a plump woman with frizzy black hair, crazy big eyeglasses, and buck teeth, Yes, buck-friggin teeth. She didn't have the advantage of growing a beard like me, so the teeth were necessary to change the appearance of her pretty face. We both requested that we didn't wear heavy face makeup, which can be a bitch when the temperature soars. As intimately as I knew her, I could pass her by in the street and not realize she was my Bobbie. Like her, I also had dark-rimmed glasses. These makeup people know what they're doing.

Bobbie looked at me and didn't even laugh.

"You thtill look gorgeouth, baby," she lisped through her new false teeth. I honestly couldn't say the same about her. I briefly thought about how pleasant it would be when we returned home at night and could remove our padding—and Bobbie's buck teeth. We looked forward to our new adventure. If I wrote an autobiography about Bobbie and me, the word dull would never appear.

CHAPTER SEVENTEEN

Bobbie

B ob and I boarded our flight at JFK, due to arrive at O'Hare Airport at 2:50. Bob stared at me, but I don't think he was admiring my normally pretty puss. I couldn't believe they gave me buck teeth. Not only were they ugly, but they interfered with eating, not to mention talking. I now thpeak with a lithp. I guess I'll lose weight, but you will never know it because of my body padding. I kept reminding myself that we need to look at this as an adventure, not just a detective assignment. Bob and I love to help each other out of our clothing at night. With all this padding crap, it will be a special pleasure.

Our FBI car picked us up outside the terminal at O'Hare. I insisted that it *not* be a big black SUV. Nothing says "Hi, I'm from the government," louder that a big black SUV. It was a burgundy Nissan sedan. We drove up to a beautiful large house in Evanston, a suburb on the northern border of Chicago. Chicago and its surrounding suburbs are often known as "Chicagoland."

Our cover story, as it was leaked to our neighbors, was that we were professors of criminology at Northwestern University, Mr. George Fleming and Mrs. Nancy Fleming. Sarah Watson's people did a perfect job of forging our credentials and lining us up with the part-time teaching jobs. What didn't need forging was our knowledge. Bob and I are more than intellectually equipped to teach criminology at a university, as we both have done from time to time over the years, me at the University of Chicago and Bob at NYU. Classes would start in two weeks, so we had time to familiarize ourselves with the textbooks.

Our huge temporary multi-family home came with seven bedrooms, including four separate full suites. Bob and I would inhabit a suite on the second floor, with our four bodyguards scattered over the others. Our suite covered the entire floor, we were happy to see. It included two bedrooms, three bathrooms, a small kitchen, a den, a dining room, and, thank goodness, a small gym.

Tom Blackburn, the guy in charge of our security detail, invited us to have supper with him and the rest of the group. He politely emphasized that it was only an invitation, and that we were more than welcome to dine alone upstairs if we wished. He and the other guys get it. Privacy is important, especially if you're undercover. But Bob and I took him up on his offer to dine with them. We wanted to get to know the men in charge of keeping us alive and safe. Also, these guys were highly trained FBI agents, so bouncing ideas off them seemed like a good idea.

None of our bodyguards were from New York or Chicago, better to keep their identities hidden. Sarah Watson knows what she's doing.

But first we wanted to go upstairs and get out of our friggin padding, not to mention my buck teeth.

Tom Blackburn didn't' miss a trick. He gave us all name badges and reminded everybody that Bob and I were George and Nancy Fleming, and that we should be addressed that way at all times. He's right. When you're undercover, your job is to *stay* undercover. We had a great supper. Agent Tim Holloway loves to cook and he's great at it. I was happy that we had a good cook among us. Of my many talents, cooking isn't one of them. Bob often tells me that I make excellent reservations. All the guys were dying to know about the adventures of Bob and Bobbie (George and Nancy?), the famous BBs. We had fun sharing our war stories with our bodyguards.

The next day, Bob and I planned to visit *Santoro's*, a restaurant in Chicago's Loop district, known to be a mob hangout. It would not be a pleasant lunch.

CHAPTER EIGHTEEN

Bob

Bobbie and I (that is, Nancy and George Fleming) taught our morning criminology classes at Northwestern University, not far from our house in Evanston. Bobbie told me she had a difficult job teaching with her false buck teeth. After our classes, we got into the car for our trip to *Santoro's*, the mob restaurant. Agent Tim Holloway would be our driver and Pete Johnston would ride shotgun. Tim punched the address into the GPS, although Bobbie could have given directions, having known Chicago like a bee knows a hive.

On the way to the restaurant, Bobbie removed her false teeth and reviewed for Tim and Pete the basic rules of "how not to look like a cop." Don't walk with your arms spread from your sides, because cops do that to avoid scraping against their sidearms. Don't sit with you back to the wall, because cops like to see what's going on. Don't stare into people's faces, because that's what cops do. Criminals know these things, and we're sure mobsters are experts at it. Have I mentioned that Bobbie knows her stuff?

The four of us walked into *Santoro*'s at 12:15. It was dark, and nicely appointed with photos on the walls. I was shocked that one of the photos was of none other than Al Capone.

We were seated at a table in the middle of the restaurant. A nearby table was occupied by six guys who spoke loudly.

"Heyy, Patsie the Peach. Heyy, Rocco the Rock. Heyy, Billy the Butch, etc. etc."

These clowns could get jobs as extras in a remake of *The Godfather*. Bobbie unobtrusively switched on her recording device and set it next to the bread dish. Bobbie affected a smile over her buck teeth, but I could tell she was seething. Like me, she's half Italian, and I knew it gnawed at her for these creeps to darken our heritage. The goombahs behind us switched to Italian. Of course, they didn't know it, but Bobbie speaks and understands Italian fluently, as she does five other languages. Bobbie is no slouch.

As we sat there, Joey the Jelly, Mickey the Mooch, and Louie the Lou, joined the group behind us, and immediately began to speak Italian. They spoke in muffled tones, not knowing that Bobbie's recording device could pick up a fly fart. Suddenly one man's voice got loud. It was Mickey the Mooch. He was the apparent leader of the group, if voice volume can be used to evaluate leadership.

Suddenly Bobbie's eyes got as wide as saucers. She immediately put her hand over them and pretended to wipe her forehead, as she didn't want the boys at the next table to detect that she'd heard something important.

Knowing Bobbie as I do, I knew it *was* something important. I was dying to hear what she had to say later after she removed her false teeth.

I enjoyed my meal of perfectly cooked Chicken parmigiana. "How did you like your lunch, hon," I asked Bobbie.

"It thucked," she said. "I normally love eating mutthels, but thucking them out of the thells wath impothible."

CHAPTER NINETEEN

Bobbie

When we got back to Evanston after our lunch at *Santoro*'s, Bob and I couldn't wait to get out of our disguises.

"Gimme a kith, handthome," I said.

"Bobbie, your teeth?"

"Holy thit. Thorry, thweety."

I went into the bathroom, removed my lovely buck teeth, brushed my real teeth, and gargled for two minutes.

I walked out of the room and flashed Bob my best smile—with my *real* teeth.

"I think I'll call you Bucky," Bob said, laughing.

"Bobbie works fine, wiseass. Now give me that kiss, and no, not a *kith*, a kiss."

It was after five, so we all decided to have an early dinner, a light one after our luncheon feast at *Santoro*'s. Again, Bob and I ate with our bodyguards. We realized that meeting regularly with four experienced FBI agents would only help us get the job done. Our guys aren't just the muscle end of the bureau—they're all bright as hell.

I turned on my voice recorder and put the volume on high. Because the recording was all in Italian, I played it slowly and translated. I put it on hold when we got to the part where Mickey the Mooch spoke loudly.

"Hang onto your hats, guys," I said. I then resumed the recording and translated.

"Okay, boys," the Mooch said, "here's the word right from the top. This operation will now be run from Chicago. I wish old Scarface could be here (referring to one of Al Capone's nicknames). Our next item of business is to whack that motherfucker Commissioner Norquist in New York."

"Dear God," Agent Holloway yelled as he reached for his cellphone, "we've got to warn him."

"Relax, Tim," I said, "I already called the Commissioner on the secure line when I went to the ladies' room at the restaurant. Thank God I heard that Mooch guy."

"Sorry, Bobbie—I mean Nancy—I should have realized that one of the BBs got it handled."

Mickey the Mooch continued. "After we take care of Norquist, we're gonna work on the rest of the cops in the country, one by one, and sometimes 10 by 10," he said, laughing. I put the player on hold.

"Bob and I and the rest of the country thought we put an end to this shit when we stopped that huge cop-killing terror plot," I said. "Looks like it's about to start all over again. Law enforcement is beginning to look like a dangerous way to make a living." I hit the play button, and Mickey the Mooch resumed talking.

"Our job is simple, guys, but it's going to take a lot of manpower and a lot of time. Cops want to stop us. The fewer the cops, the fewer we need to worry about. Soon, only assholes will want to become cops. I'm running the show here in Chicago and Angie Dee is in charge in New York."

I put the device on hold. "Bob, do you think Angie Dee could be Angelo DiCrispino, our suspect in the *Morton Case*?"

Bob jotted down a note. I hit play.

"Who's in charge of this operation?" Patsie the Peach asked.

"I can't tell you that, Patsie. I can't tell anybody that. As we've learned over the years from the FBI and the cops, secrecy is the name of the fucking game."

The rest of the Mafia conversation concerned their loan-sharking operation in Chicago. I turned off the machine.

"What do you need from us, Bobbie, I mean Nancy?" Lead Agent Tom Blackburn asked.

"We want you guys to keep your eyes and ears open," I said. "If you think of something that may be important, Bob and I want to hear about it. You're all experienced agents, and that's why we're bringing you inside this mess. I've discussed this with Director Watson, and she has no problem with it. She handpicked you guys, so she has no concern about your knowing what's going on. But she wants to communicate directly with only Bob and me in what she calls 'executive sessions.' I'm going to call her right after this meeting. Thanks for your attention, guys. I recommend you always keep an extra bullet magazine in your pockets. Bob and I are doing just that."

CHAPTER TWENTY

Bob

After we met with our bodyguards, Bobbie and I huddled in our room to prepare for our call with Sarah Watson. We're beginning to think of our FBI agents as our *team*, not just our bodyguards. Our phone appointment with Sarah was an hour away. Bobbie had just taken a shower, and sat on the couch in her robe, her pretty little bare feet perched on an ottoman. God, she looked sexy. I walked over and stroked her face.

"Hey, handsome, can't you think of something more exciting to stroke than my face?"

"Yes, I can, but it will require you to take off your clothes."

She stood, dropped her robe, exposing her unbelievably hot body. She then reached over and reached under my robe, touching my eager love member.

We thrusted against each other, slowly at first, then picking up the tempo. Bobbie and I have sex so often, we've become experts at arousing each other. We came to a mutual exploding orgasm, the *Mountaintop*, as we love to call it. We bit on the pillow to keep our screams from our bodyguards downstairs.

Forty-five minutes later, Bobbie reminded me of our phone

appointment with Sarah Watson in 15 minutes. We lay together, our naked bodies entwined. We took a quick shower, but not too quick to stop us from making love again.

Stakeout duty has its benefits.

The phone rang, and it was Sarah.

"With all the work you two have been doing, I hope you've found a way to relax."

"Yes, Sarah, we've found a way to relax," Bobbie said as she stroked my thigh.

Bobbie reviewed our eavesdropping lunch and gave Sarah a blow-by-blow account of what we heard. Sarah shocked the living shit out of us by saying that there had, indeed, been an assassination attempt on Commissioner Norquist that afternoon. Thanks to Bobbie's warning call, the would-be-assassin was killed before he could get off a round. How the hell can a guy with a loaded gun enter One Police Plaza? Looks like we're up against a tough enemy, an extremely tough enemy.

The thought crossed my mind that if it weren't for Bobbie's fluency in Italian, our day would have consisted of nothing more than a tasty meal. And, thank God, Mickey the Mooch spoke loudly about assassinating Norquist. If we needed to wait to hear Bobbie translate it from the recorder, Ralph would be dead.

"Bob and Bobbie," Sarah said, "Do you have any idea how high-up in the organization these men were?"

"Only that the guy who they call Mickey the Mooch was in charge of the meeting," Bobbie said. "We didn't get any of their last names, only the stupid mob nicknames they give themselves. Have you ever heard of Mickey the Mooch?"

"Yes, Bobbie, I'm quite familiar with Mickey the Mooch. His

name is Michael Marcado, and he's been a lynchpin in the Chicago Mob for years. He's a very dangerous man. Any time you're near him, make sure the safety's off on your guns."

"Sarah, does the name 'Angie Dee' ring a bell with you?" I asked.

"Yes, he's Angelo DiCrispino, a mob enforcer in New York. Was he there?"

"No, but we heard his name. He's a suspect in a murder case that Bobbie and I were working on in New York."

We went over all the names of the mobsters with Sarah and then reviewed our plan for our next action, the next restaurant for lunch. These mobsters like to eat well.

CHAPTER TWENTY-ONE

Bobbie

After we heard the chilling words of Mickey the Mooch yesterday, we were all on heightened security. Our FBI guys all sported M16s strapped to their shoulders as well as their regular sidearms in their holsters. Our house—the safe house—was decked out like a military base. The entire perimeter was covered by wireless motion alarms, and one of the agents would man a security camera on a rotating basis. By touching different buttons, the agent could see every square foot of the property surrounding the house. Every window and door in the house was protected by motion detectors.

Sarah had secured three vehicles for us, realizing that one car for six people would raise eyebrows. At my urging again, none of the vehicles was a big black SUV, as sure a sign of government as a tattoo on a gang member. We had a red Ford Expedition, a beige Chevy Suburban, and a green Toyota Land Cruiser. All the vehicles were large, in the event that all six of us needed to go somewhere together.

Today's destination was *Venicia*, an Italian restaurant in the Rogers Park section of Chicago, right near Evanston, another place that intelligence indicated was populated by mobsters. To avoid people seeing us move as a group, only two agents accompanied

Bob and me for lunch.

As soon as we walked in, we saw a group of men seated at a table in back. They looked like goombahs. Being part Italian myself, that's probably an inappropriate thing to say, but sorry, they looked like *goombahs*.

The *maître d* led us to a table about 20 feet from the group of men. No way would we ask to be seated closer to them, as that may arouse suspicions. No problem. My listening device is so sensitive it can pick up voices from across a large room. As wise guy Bob says, my device can pick up a fly fart. I nicknamed the device, Big Ears. I set it next to a water pitcher and pointed the recording end toward the goombah table. Bob looked at me, smiled and winked. I flashed him my best buck-toothy smile. I leaned over and whispered in his ear. "Hey, baby, tonight let's do a repeat performance of last night."

He kissed me on my ear, causing my girlie parts to flip. "Yes, honey, we have a date for tonight. Do we ever."

Okay, time to get to work.

Unlike our lunch yesterday at *Santoro's,* we weren't close enough to hear the conversation, but would need to rely on my device to record the words and do our listening later.

We all spent a long few minutes perusing the menu to buy us some time. If the boys in the back are anything like yesterday, they weren't just there for lunch but for a meeting. We asked the waiter detailed questions about the menu. When Bob asked the waiter what the chicken parmigiana was made from, the guy looked confused and said, "chicken." We all cracked up, which was the purpose of Bob's question. The more we laugh the less we look like cops. It takes a lot of thinking to be a good detective.

We ate as slowly as we could, noticing that the goombahs were taking their sweet time, sipping sambuca. To take up more time, we all ordered dessert, fruit plates only. The tables around us emptied, making us begin to look conspicuous. Well, this is a scouting operation, so we can skip a few things the boys were talking about, I figured. I scribbled a note to Bob, suggesting that we hit the road. He nodded in agreement. As we got up, Agent Pete Johnston cracked a really funny joke. We laughed hysterically, trying to look as un-cop as possible.

We got back to Evanston at 4 p.m., having spent a long time at lunch. How do these mobsters find anything else to do besides endless lunch meetings? We couldn't wait to listen to Big Ears.

We were in for a shock.

CHAPTER TWENTY-TWO

Bob

L ike all people, detectives need to brace themselves for occasional disappointment. When we got back from *Venicia*, we listened with excitement as Bobbie prepared to translate the conversation her device had recorded.

The "goombahs" we spied on were Little League soccer coaches and met to discuss the upcoming playoffs. They spoke English, not a word of Italian, so Bobbie didn't even need to translate. Our eavesdropping lunch was nothing but a waste of time. We laughed. There was nothing else to do. Just as with any surveillance operation, you need to brace yourself for frustration, which was definitely what today was all about—frustration. Bobbie and I flipped a coin to see who would use the gym in our apartment first. We didn't want our luncheon routines to hit our waistlines. Bobbie won the toss, and we went to our apartment.

After we removed our pads, and Bobbie's false teeth, she put on her sweat suit and hit the gym. I love to watch Bobbie work out. It's no wonder she has such a gorgeous figure.

As Bobbie took a shower, I began my workout, feeling good that I'd at least accomplish something today.

After I showered, I walked into the den wearing my robe. Bobbie was lying on the couch, reading a magazine. She stood, smiled, and dropped her robe to the floor, exposing her beautiful naked body. The frustrations of today suddenly disappeared. We began our second workout of the day. I love to see my chubby buck-toothed partner transform into a gorgeous, sexy blond after hours.

CHAPTER TWENTY-THREE

Bobbie

I f somebody asks me what I do for a living, I could honestly say, "I have lunch." I recognize that, as a detective, I need to do things that are productive and can lead to solving a case. Eating lunch at a known hangout of Mafia types only makes sense. Yes, it can sometimes be frustrating, as yesterday when we discovered that we recorded a bunch of Little League soccer coaches talking shop. So what. Frustration is part of the job, something you need to live with. The day before yesterday we hit pay dirt, so sometimes it works.

Today we plan to have lunch at *Pietro*'s, an Italian restaurant in the Bridgeport area of Chicago where the late Mayor Daly used to live. Agents Pete Johnston and Tom Blackburn would accompany us today, with Tom driving the Ford Expedition. According to the intelligence reports we read, *Pietro*'s festers with mobsters. It was raining slightly, doing wonders for my already-frizzy black-dyed wig. At least it wouldn't bother my beautiful buck teeth.

"My, you look lovely today," Bob the wiseass said.

"Thame to you, thweety," my teeth said.

The hostess seated us next to a table of eight men. Because intelligence tells us this is a goombah hangout, maybe we'll get lucky. I placed Big Ears, my recording device, next to the bread dish. Bread, just what I need. I aimed the mic of Big Ears toward the next table.

Bob looked down at a sheet of paper and recited a funny joke, cracking us all up, and announcing to anyone listening that we're not police.

They spoke Italian. Although my device would record their every word, I strained to hear if they were saying anything interesting. They spoke softly, so I couldn't pick up much. That's what Big Ears is for. But I did hear one name mentioned over and over—Mickey the Mooch. The Mooch was not at this meeting. A guy named Billy the Butch was doing most of the talking. If I heard the Italian word for "whacked" once, I heard it a dozen times. I thought our listening session tonight would be interesting.

They kept talking about some guy named Bobbo the Bob. Cute name. Maybe I'll nickname my partner that. It seems that Bobbo the Bob had just arrived from New York, and he announced some big plans, which I didn't catch, but would later. According to Billy the Butch, Bobbo the Bob would join them later. Looks like we're going to need to eat quite slowly.

As we ate our lunch, we cracked jokes to make us laugh. A tall overweight man walked up to the table next to us, whom we would soon learn was Bobbo the Bob. "Heyy, Bobbo the Bob; Heyy, Billy the Butch; Heyy, Tony the Tank," etc., etc. Maybe I'll change my name to Bobbie the Bitch. One man took up almost the entire end of the table. Tony the Tank was built just like that, an army tank, a fat army tank.

After their charming hellos, they all resumed speaking Italian. I could give them lessons on proper Italian, but I don't think they'd be interested. I noticed they spoke in hushed tones, but not too hushed for my Big Ears device. I did hear the name Mickey the Mooch repeated constantly. Apparently, Mickey the Mooch is a popular topic of conversation.

As we slowly finished our fruit cup desserts, the goombahs arose and started to walk out. We waited for five minutes after they left and then we walked to our car. From the snippets of conversation I caught, I knew our meeting this evening would be productive.

As we pulled up to the house in Evanston, Tim pressed a button on the dashboard, causing the gate to swing open.

Bob and I went to our apartment to get undisguised, especially my goddam buck teeth. Because we didn't have much time, Bob and I hugged each other and made out—for only five minutes.

We all gathered in the kitchen for my translation. Tom Blackburn stood by a window holding his M16. Tim Holloway, our resident FBI chef, prepared a chicken dish, light on carbs. Because we spend so much time eating on our surveillance gigs, Tim makes sure to watch the calories and carbs on the meals he prepares.

I played the recording and began to translate. I recited aloud anything that sounded interesting, leaving out stuff like, "Hey, try the lasagna, it's fucking great."

The guys seemed to hang on every word of my translation, and so did I because this was the first time I heard the conversation clearly.

Holy shit, what did I just hear? I backed up and hit play again.

"Mickey the Mooch says the Big Guy isn't happy with the speed of things," Bobbo the Bob said. "We whacked five cops in New York this morning, but the boss says that's not enough." I put it on hold. "Did you guys catch what I just translated? Five dead cops in New York just this morning."

The secure phone rang, and Tim picked up.

"It's Director Watson."

"Hi, Sarah, can I put you on speaker?"

"Yes, please do," Sarah said, "I want everyone to hear this. I just got off the phone with Commissioner Norquist in New York. Five policemen were assassinated this morning. He just found out about it."

"He just found out about it? I was just translating our eavesdropping session today, and one of the men mentioned the assassinations. I recommend, Sarah, that you stay on the line and listen to my translation. It will take a while."

"I have absolutely nothing more important to do, Bobbie, please continue."

I repeated my translation of Bobbo the Bob saying that Mickey the Mooch announced that somebody he referred to as "The Big Guy" wanted the cop killings to speed up. He mentioned that five cops were whacked in New York this morning.

I hit play and continued to translate. Almost everything we heard was important, with no more analysis of the taste of the lasagna.

"The Big Guy says he likes the number 10," Bobbo the Bob said. "He wants to see 10 cops whacked in one day in one city, this time in Chicago. Once that's done, the Big Guy wants every hit to be 10 at the minimum, with a bonus offered for anything over that number."

"Please put it on hold Bobbie, I'll be right back." Sarah said.

We all knew what she was about to do. She wanted to warn the Chicago police chief about what she heard. She came back on the line.

"I just had my deputy contact the Chicago Police Superintendent about the threat. I hope it's not too late. Please continue, Bobbie."

"As you guys know," Bobbo the Bob said, "Mickey the Mooch

runs the show in Chicago. When the Big Guy wants something handled, get out of Mickey's way because he'll get it fucking done."

Bob motioned to me and I put Big Ears on hold.

"Sarah, do you have any idea who this Big Guy is?" Bob asked.

"We're not certain, but we think it's Alphonse Gandolfo, head of the Gandolfo family in New York. He's a vicious son of a bitch. We'll know more as the days go by. Since you BBs have been on this case, I've signed more wiretap warrant applications than I have in the past year. Please continue, Bobbie."

Tony the Tank spoke, his mouth half-full of pasta.

"When Mickey the Mooch says jump, I say how high. I'm going to turn my people loose on this today. Ten cops? Shit, that's nothing. And I like the idea of a bonus for more than 10. The Big Guy knows what he's doing, and so does Mickey the Mooch. We'll get this fucking thing done. I know *I* will."

"When is this supposed to happen?" Billy the Butch asked.

"Both the Big Guy and Mickey the Mooch want it to happen tomorrow, beginning in the morning," Bobbo the Bob said.

"Please hold, Bobbie. I'll be right back," Sarah said.

When she came back on the line, we all knew what she did. She had her deputy warn the Chicago Police Superintendent about the newly-announced timing of the attacks. But even though Sarah was able to sound the warning to the Chicago police chief, what could he do? The Chicago Police Department employs 12,000 cops. Should they all walk around with their guns drawn?

I went through the remainder of the recording, with nothing much more than what we already heard. And we heard plenty. Just as in the big terrorist case that Bob and I handled, the police departments of the country are under attack.

Sarah Watson signed off and told us to call her immediately about anything new we learned.

This crap was starting to get scary, real scary.

CHAPTER TWENTY-FOUR

Y ou wanted to see me, Don Gandolfo?"

"Look at these photos, Vincenzo. Tony Pasquarelli took them. The two chubby people you're looking at are detectives with the NYPD. They've been deputized as FBI agents, and are in Chicago to spy on us. Every day they have lunch at one of the restaurants where our people hang out. The two are married. Ever hear the names Bobbie Nelson and Bob Lawton?"

"Yeah, aren't those two the famous detectives who have been in magazines and on the news?"

"Yes, they are, Vincenzo. That buck-toothed fat lady you're looking at is none other than Detective Bobbie Nelson, one of the hottest pieces of ass I've ever seen. When she worked in Chicago, the *Chicago Tribune* carried an article about her, calling her a real-life Sherlock Holmes. She may be a hot fox, but she's one tough cop. And the fat guy with her is her husband, Detective Bob Lawton, a slim muscular guy with dark brown hair, not the chubby blond you're looking at. And he doesn't wear a beard. So, they've disguised some high-powered people and sent them to spy on us."

"Do we know where they're staying, Don Gandolfo?"

"Yeah, a place in Evanston, which the idiots think is a safe house.

Here's the address."

"Do you want me to take care of them?"

"No, I don't want them whacked—not just yet. I want them followed so we can find out what they're up to. I had one of my people rent an apartment across the street from where they're staying. I want you to stay there and watch the house carefully. When they leave the house, I want you to follow them. You're good at tailing cars."

"I'll go there today, Don Gandolfo."

"This is an important job, Vincenzo. Do it right and I'll take good care of you."

CHAPTER TWENTY-FIVE

Bob

B obbie and I went up to our apartment after the big listening session with Sarah Watson. We sat in the den, sipping a couple of martinis I had mixed for us.

"Bob, this shit is even worse than the terror attacks on police. The Mafia has become more organized than they've ever been, and they have every reason to kill cops, which they're probably doing as we speak."

"Not only does the mob have a reason to kill cops in general—they have every reason in the world to kill you and me, Bobbie. Sarah Watson convinced us to come out of the Witness Protection Program, but I'm beginning to question the wisdom of that move. Every day, we have lunch at another gangster hangout, and every day I wonder how long we can continue without being spotted."

I really need to stop this crap. We're getting results, big results as Bobbie and I always do, and soon the results will start to show in the statistics. The important thing is that we're uncovering names and giving them to the FBI, along with our recordings. I can easily see that in the near future, our recording sessions will be put into evidence when these bastards are prosecuted. The one name we haven't gotten is the real name for The Big Guy, although Sarah

Watson thinks it's Alphonse Gandolfo, head of the Gandolfo family in New York. Unlike the old days of mob activity, this new reality sees a lot of cooperation not only among the families, but also between different states and cities. As Sarah Watson has observed, the Mafia is becoming modern and corporate in its structure.

"Hey, Bobbie," I said. "you're looking pensive tonight."

"Yeah, I'm pensive because I'm worried, Bob. I'm worried because I think we're making a stupid assumption. Want to guess what it is?"

"Yeah, our stupid assumption is that the mob leadership is stupid. We spy on them and assume they don't know they're being spied upon."

"Exactly. Our disguise costumes are good, but maybe *too* good. We're easy to pick out of a crowd, me with my friggin buck teeth and you with your blond hair and beard. The first time some of the mob people see us, no problem, but what about the next time? Sarah has given us 27 restaurants where mob bosses hang out. Can we believe that they never have lunch at a different place? If so, what happens if they remember seeing us at another restaurant? I think we need to train a lot of agents to eavesdrop, which isn't rocket science. All they need to do is what we do— Sit and try not to look or act like cops and point a recording device like Big Ears toward a group of suspects. That's it. I can still do the translating if the targets speak Italian, but I don't need to be on-site at a lunch place, and neither do you. And the agents should be rotated regularly so that they never visit the same restaurant twice."

"I think you're right, honey. If we spend all our time visiting mob hangouts, it's only a matter of time for somebody to recognize us. Those creeps may sound stupid, but they're not."

The phone rang. It was Sarah Watson. The time was 8:30 p.m.

"Don't leave the house," Sarah said loudly. "We've intercepted some emails accompanied by photos of you two in your disguises, along with photos of you without the disguises. Two pictures were taken at two different restaurants. Bottom line—the mob is on to you. Your cover is blown, completely blown. The restaurants you've visited have given us valuable names and leads, but those sources have just dried up."

"Bobbie and I have been worried about exactly that, Sarah. I'm putting you on speaker. My amazing partner sitting next to me has come up with a new idea."

Bobbie explained her plan, which is to use a large number of agents and rotate them so they never show up more than once at a mob restaurant. Because, as Sarah put it, our cover is blown, Bobbie's plan is not just a good idea, it's essential—unless we want to get killed.

Sarah told us she'd call again in the morning.

CHAPTER TWENTY-SIX

Bobbie

Bob and I didn't get much sleep last night, and it wasn't because we were feeling frisky. We couldn't sleep because of what Sarah Watson told us yesterday. Not only is our cover blown, but the mob has photos of us in our disguises, and also *without* our disguises. I felt like I was walking along the edge of a tall building with no railing to hold. Tom Blackburn, our lead bodyguard, ordered the other three agents to carry an M16 at all times, and reminded us to always wear our service revolvers except while sleeping. He continuously monitored the yard on the surveillance camera.

At 8:45 a.m. Sarah Watson called. I put her on speaker.

"I'm about to tell you two what you already know. We've got to get you back into the Witness Protection Program. You'll fly to New York tomorrow and we'll meet you at JFK. I'm sending one of our makeup artists to you this afternoon so you will have different disguises. Don't worry, you won't need to wear heavy padding, and Bobbie won't wear false teeth. Sorry, folks, but your covers are so blown that I refuse to leave you there in danger of your lives."

Our makeup artist arrived an hour later. She shaved off Bob's beard, gave him a short haircut and died it black. She did mine into a pixie cut. No false teeth, thank God. She then handed us two naval officer's uniforms. Interesting disguises, but the uniforms didn't change our faces.

Bob's stripes were those of a lieutenant commander, and mine were those of a lieutenant. I hoped he wouldn't order me to salute him. We weren't excited about the idea of returning to friendly prisoner status in the Witness Protection Program, but we sure as hell were happy to be leaving Illinois and our shortened life expectancies. Bob and I drafted a set of instructions for our replacement spies. It was simple, really, because there wasn't much to do except sit at a table with a recording device and try not to look like law enforcement.

Bob and I love our work as detectives, we love *Detectiving,* but we hated to be on the run and hunted.

This shit is getting old.

CHAPTER TWENTY-SEVEN

Bob

B obbie and I, along with all four of our FBI bodyguards, arrived at O'Hare Airport at 1 p.m. for our flight to JFK in New York, which would depart at 3:05. We sported our naval officer uniforms, which I thought was a smart move on Sarah's part, even though as a former Marine officer I felt out of place. But it beats my blond hair and beard. But I was worried, as was Bobbie, that it didn't change the appearance of our faces, and, as Sarah told us, the mob knows what we looked like before the disguises. Our disguise artists did their best to cloak our faces with heavy makeup. Soon we'll be out of here and on our way to New York.

After we checked in, all six of us went to our boarding area. The agents' FBI identification enabled them to accompany us to the departure gate. Bobbie and I agreed that we'd miss these guys, who had become friends, not just bodyguards.

Bobbie announced that she needed to use the ladies' room. Tom Blackburn and Pete Johnston stationed themselves on either side of the ladies' room door.

Ten minutes went by, then twenty.

I was worried that Bobbie may be sick. I walked over to Tom

Blackburn and said, "I think we need to check on Bobbie." I felt my stomach twist.

He flagged down a woman wearing the uniform of a TSA agent, flashed his FBI badge, and said, "Please check on a woman in a naval officer's uniform. She's been in there a long time and we're worried she may be ill."

One minute later the woman came back out.

"There is no woman in a naval officer's uniform in there," she said.

"We're going in," I said.

The TSA woman said, "I'll go with you." When we walked in, she shouted, "Police business, everybody stand where you are." Sharp lady.

But the room was empty. The agent told us she had to knock down a makeshift barricade to enter the first time.

I pointed toward a hatch about two feet above floor level.

"Where does that lead?" I asked. By that time a couple of airport cops had entered.

"That leads to a conveyor belt that goes to a storage room," one of the cops said.

I unholstered my Glock.

"Hey, what the hell is that about?"

I flashed my NYPD shield and said, "Long story." He looked at my Navy stripes, then at my shield, then at my gun.

"Pete and I will go," Tom said, "then you can follow us, Bob."

We climbed through the hatch and positioned ourselves on the conveyor belt for our journey to the storage room. As my mind was freaking out, I tried to flip into detective mode, and scoured the walls of the tunnel for anything that could provide a clue to Bobbie's whereabouts. Nothing.

I called Sarah Watson to let her know what happened. Within minutes, the airport was covered with FBI agents. Where the hell could Bobbie be?

CHAPTER TWENTY-EIGHT

Bobbie

Great, simply fucking great. I was washing my hands in the ladies' room when two women, best described as Amazons, grabbed me by my arms. Each of them was just shy of six feet and had the shoulders of a linebacker. I noticed a third woman, wearing a cleaning uniform, barricade the entrance to the ladies' room from the inside. Amazon Number One crawled through a hatch in the wall and Amazon Number Two pushed me in behind her. Then, Amazon Number Two climbed in behind me, followed by the cleaning lady.

We sat on a conveyor belt which took us through a tunnel. After a couple of minutes, we were deposited in what looked like a storage room. I immediately noticed that the room was empty. By this time, they had removed my pistol, handcuffed me, and put tape over my mouth. They pushed me toward a door, which opened next to a SUV. I was told to lie on the floor and keep my mouth shut. Keeping my mouth shut was easy because it was taped.

After what I estimated was a half-hour, the vehicle stopped. Amazon Number One yanked me off the floor and shoved a fabric bag over my head while Amazon Number Two dragged me out of the SUV. We went into what I assumed was a house because we had to climb four steps to enter. I was pushed into a seat as Amazon

Number One pulled the bag off my head. We were in a suburban kitchen.

My hands were cuffed in front of me, not behind my back. *BIG MISTAKE.*

"Mickey will be here in a half-hour," Amazon Number One said to Amazon Number Two in Italian, obviously not knowing that I speak the language. I wondered if she was referring to Mickey the Mooch. I had one simple set of objectives as I had been trained—to remain calm, observe what was going on, and wait for an opening. Although I had fired a gun only once in the line of duty, when I killed the guy who shot Bob, I had a ton of training over the years, including training for a situation just like this—being held prisoner.

I noticed that Amazon Number One had placed her gun on a side table, about ten feet from where I sat. I couldn't believe she did that, and I struggled to keep an expression of shock from my face. I'm quite an athlete, as Bob always reminds me, and I can move fast. I noticed that Amazon Number Two stood there with her arms folded in front of her. The cleaning lady, meanwhile, had driven off.

In two quick strides I reached the side table, grabbed the gun, flipped off the safety, and fired two rounds into the torso of Amazon Number One. I then did the same for Amazon Number Two as she reached for her gun. They both lay dead on the kitchen floor. I ripped the tape off my mouth, which was tricky because my hands were cuffed together. It hurt like hell. I grabbed my cellphone from the pocket of Amazon Number Two and got the location of the house from Google Maps. Then I called Bob. He didn't say hello, he just screamed my name. I didn't have a moment to waste because Mickey (the Mooch?) would be arriving shortly. I gave Bob the location from my phone. That's all I needed to do. Bob's one hell of a cop, and he'd take it from there. Within four minutes, I heard two police sirens. I stood on the front stoop with my cuffed hands in the air. Crime scenes can be fluid and scary, and I didn't want to risk getting shot—again. As two of the cops unspooled crime scene tape around the place, the other two questioned me in the front parlor, away from the bloody kitchen. One of the cops found the handcuff keys on a chain around the neck of Amazon Number One and uncuffed me.

I answered their questions slowly and deliberately, being careful not to provide too much information. I'm sure Sarah Watson wants to treat this whole matter with the utmost secrecy. Ten minutes later, Bob and the FBI agents walked up to the door, hooking their badges onto their jackets. I'm sure the cops who questioned me must have freaked out. Here they were questioning a woman naval officer who had just showed them her NYPD shield, hugging another naval officer who had just shown them his. Bob and I hugged for the longest time I could remember, and we hug a lot. I asked him not to kiss me because my lower lip was bleeding from my ripping the fucking tape off.

Mickey (the Mooch?) never showed up.

Bob had already spoken to Sarah, who arranged for an FBI Gulfstream to meet us at the airport.

"A Gulfstream?" I said to Bob. "Maybe we can draw the curtain and play around." I figured a dumb little wisecrack was called for. I was keeping it all together, or at least I tried. Later I would break down into hysterical tears on the plane as Bob held me in his arms. I pride myself on being a tough cop, but I had come closer than I ever had to being killed. Not a pleasant feeling, even for a "tough cop."

CHAPTER TWENTY-NINE

Bob

My stiff upper lip was beginning to quiver. Bobbie, *my Bobbie*, was almost fucking killed. If she wasn't such a well-toned jock, that's exactly what would have happened. The mob would have pumped her for information and then knocked her off, as Mickey the Mooch and the Big Guy are fond of doing.

When we got to the Witness Protection Program location, Sarah Watson was there waiting for us. It was a beautiful house in Tenafly, New Jersey, an upscale suburb not far from Manhattan. It was surrounded by trees, a security fence, and a large defensible lawn. When we walked in, Sarah broke down in tears and hugged Bobbie. Then she hugged me. Yes, tough-as-nails FBI Director Watson cried.

"Bobbie's brief kidnapping has the entire bureau on crisis alert. My God, it's hard to believe what happened. To abduct someone from a ladies' room at a crowded airport shows a new level of brazenness. Chutzpah should be a Sicilian word. It was my idea to put you two into disguises so you could spy up-close. We, including myself, didn't realize the sophistication of this newborn mob. Never did we imagine that they'd station people at their favorite restaurants to see if they're being observed. This isn't the old mob, not by any stretch."

"Sarah, just tell me one thing. I won't need to wear buck teeth here, will I?" Bobbie said.

Sarah cracked up.

"No, you won't be wearing disguises here. I know that you two got restless the last time you were in WPP, but this time it will be different. You will be working the intellectual side of law enforcement, helping us design systems and new methods of surveillance."

———

Bobbie and I aren't emotionally constituted for inactivity, and Sarah's idea that we would work the "intellectual side of law enforcement" wasn't doing it for us. Bobbie's translating worked wonders, of course, but she isn't the only law enforcement agent who speaks and understands Italian. Dozens of FBI agents know the language, we're sure, not to mention people in the NYPD, so translating shouldn't be a problem. We needed to be outside the Witness Protection Program, and we politely requested that Sarah make it happen. We reminded Sarah of her excellent idea of disguising us as naval officers. But then Sarah reminded *us* that Bobbie was kidnapped and almost killed—in a Navy uniform. We realized that if we left the safety of the WPP, we would need disguises again, but not pads and buck teeth. Bobbie was a particular problem. Without buck teeth, her gorgeous face would stand out in a crowd, especially a crowd that knows our identities. I can always grow a beard and change its color from time to time. Sarah also reminded us that nobody, including Bobbie and me, had any idea how the mob figured out we'd be at O'Hare Airport that day. Sarah suspected, as did we, that the information had to come from only one place—inside. Not a comforting thought, but a realistic one. A bad cop had spied on us.

Bobbie came up with a new idea. We would dress as clergy, Catholic clergy. I'm going to be a priest, and Bobbie a nun. Even the goombahs, who see religion as some sort of mystical cult, would be hesitant to whack a person of the cloth. Would it work? We still can't be seen together all the time at the same restaurants, looking like a couple of religious people dating. We figured the only way to make it work would be for us to split up, and not dine at a mob restaurant together. But for our first excursion we would go together. Bobbie would be partnered with a woman FBI undercover agent, also dressed as a nun. I would wear a gray wig. Just as we learned in Chicago, we couldn't go to the same restaurant more than once but would switch off with other agents. In New York, the FBI identified 15 restaurants as mob-friendly places. For our first outing we would go as four, two priests, including me and an FBI agent, and Bobbie and another agent, the nuns. It took some doing to find the right religious habit for Bobbie so as not to accentuate her generous boobs. She wore the severe old-fashioned habit of the Dominican order. I couldn't help laughing, having just recalled that I made passionate love to this nun a few hours ago.

The first restaurant we chose was *Francesco's* on the lower East Side. We were fortunate to be seated at a table next to one with eight men, a possible mob meeting. We bowed our heads in prayer to say grace before meals. Bobbie carefully placed Big Ears with the mic toward the table next to us. As always, we told a lot of jokes so we could assume a non-cop appearance with our laughter. The meeting next to us was conducted in hushed tones, leading us to hope that some serious stuff was being discussed. Then we recalled our lunch in Chicago where we sat next to the Little League soccer coaches, who spoke softly. As always, the evening translation would tell us whether we had a productive outing or not.

Later we would learn, just as with the soccer coaches in Chicago, our eavesdropping that day was a waste of time. The group we spied on was a Kiwanis Club meeting.

CHAPTER THIRTY

Bob

Bobbie and I sat in the den of our safe house in Tenafly, New Jersey, reading the Sunday *New York Times* as we sipped coffee. Bobbie had just opened the *Book Review* section.

"Holy shit," she screamed. "Bob, we hit the non-fiction *Best Seller List* at number two. *Detectiving* is a best seller, a best-friggin-seller! Gimme a hug, baby."

Bobbie the jock then did three cartwheels and a handstand.

The secure phone rang. It was Ralph Norquist. I put him on speaker.

"I am so fucking proud of you two, I can't stand it," he said. "My two best detectives are best-selling authors. Well, I wish you *were* my detectives, which you will once again be after you get out of that goddam Witness Protection Program. I read your book cover to cover. *Detectiving* is the best damn book on detective work ever written, and the BBs got it done, which is no surprise."

If we weren't in the WPP, I'm sure we would have a day full of congratulatory phone calls, but, because our phone number is secret, they were mainly secure emails. Buster called from the CIA, and, of course, Sarah Watson from the FBI. What floored us was a call from

President Fenton and First Lady Meg.

We enjoyed our day in the sun, even though we couldn't venture forth without disguises. I can't believe we're best-selling authors. What can be better news than this?

The next day we'd find out.

CHAPTER THIRTY-ONE

Bobbie

S arah Watson's in town, Bob. She just called and says she wants to see us, and get this—for the first time that I can recall, she sounded happy as hell about something. She had already called yesterday to congratulate us on our book hitting the best-seller list, so it must be something else."

We weren't planning any religious-garbed stakeouts that day, and therefore we weren't dressed as clergy, just blue jeans and NYPD sweatshirts. Bob and I agreed that we were getting fed up with this stakeout crap in disguises. It got me kidnapped in Chicago, and we figured it was just a matter of time until the mob figures us out and blows our cover again. We wished to hell that we could go back to doing what we we're good at—*Detectiving*. But, because Mafia management was on to us, we needed to live in a safe house and venture forth only when disguised. This sucks.

At 11 a.m. Sarah Watson was escorted into our den by one of our bodyguards. She wore the biggest smile I had ever seen on her.

"I'll get right to the point," she said, still smiling. "We've decapitated the Mafia. Welcome back to a normal life. You two have earned it. The following gentlemen are safely in custody of the Justice Department: Mickey the Mooch, Bobbo the Bob, Tony the

Tank, Angie Dee, and a few dozen others, the most significant of whom is none other than Alphonse Gandolfo, better known as the Big Guy. In a plea bargain, they even coughed up the name of the cop who ratted you out. Thanks to your efforts, we have a mountain, and I do mean a mountain of evidence against them, including solid facts pointing toward first degree murder convictions. You no longer need to worry about your covers being blown. Rick Bellamy told me his wife wants to have you on *The Ellen Bellamy Show* again. Yes, you can once again be on national TV. You guys can stop wearing disguises. Welcome back to freedom."

We each took turns hugging Sarah, and then hugged each other. This news was right up there with our book becoming a best seller.

So, we're free. No more Witness Protection Program. No more disguises. No more Bobbie in buck teeth. Our safe house in Tenafly was lovely, but we both knew it was a lovely prison. I felt like I was breathing in fresh ocean air, just like our waterfront home in East Hampton. We're free!

CHAPTER THIRTY-TWO

Bob

I know you've heard me say this before," Commissioner Ralph said, "but you two are unbelievable, just fucking unbelievable. You guys spied on the mob, which has now been decapitated. When I call you NYPD royalty I mean it."

Bobbie and I have long ago started to think of Ralph Norquist as a friend, not just a boss. He sure isn't afraid to throw around flattery. Come to think of it, I believe his flattery is justified.

"We got a major assist from Bennie Weinberg," I said. "That is one shrink who knows his stuff."

"Yes, Bennie's a great guy and perceptive as hell, but you two nailed it by good old-fashioned detective work. For the next edition of your book, you should add this as a chapter."

"So, Ralph, can Bob and I take a few days off, or do you have another big case for us to handle?"

"Of course, you can take a few days off, and enjoy your beach house in East Hampton. And, in answer to your alternate question, yes, of course I have another huge case for you two to handle."

He handed me a file, a thick file.

"The mob assignment was a walk in the park compared to this shit," Ralph said.

"Tell me it's another serial killer," I said.

"Well, it's more than that, if there *can* be more than that. Yes, it involves a serial killer, but there's more than one; it's a group of serial killers, and they seem to coordinate with each other."

"Dear God," Bobbie said, "Is there one *modus operandi* of the killers?"

"Yes, in all states where the murders occurred, the killing was done by a poison dart from a dart gun," Ralph said. "And it gets worse. The poison used doesn't kill immediately. The victim takes as long as an hour to die, and the suffering is horrible."

"Are the victims men or women?"

"They're both, and they're all *schoolteachers*, 75 across the country. So far 45 women and 30 men have been killed. Some group of psychos has declared war on the American educational system."

"This is like the police terrorism case that Bob and I worked last year," Bobbie said. "How many states are involved so far?"

"Twenty states have seen teachers killed by dart guns, but the number will obviously go up."

"But how can Bob and I work cases from other states?"

"I'm not assigning these poison dart cases to you guys. I have a much bigger case for you two, much bigger," Ralph said.

The next day Bob and I hired a rental car for the trip to our beach house in East Hampton. We looked forward to some fun and relaxation.

We wondered how long that would last.

CHAPTER THIRTY-THREE

Bob

There's nothing like working a serial killing case that makes you want to take a few vacation days. Problem is, we had another serial killer file with us, but that's okay, Bobbie and I love to work cases. We also love to play around. And fresh ocean air makes for great playing around.

After we had a light lunch, Bobbie walked up to me and gave me a hug.

"Hey, handsome, we've been neglecting something important recently."

"What?"

"Us."

She squeezed me as if she thought I was going somewhere. I wasn't going anywhere. I was exactly where I wanted to be.

"Hey, Bob, what's that I feel below my waist?"

"It rhymes with election."

"Election? Sounds exciting. Hey, let's go to bed and vote."

"Think I'll win?"

"I think we'll *both* win," she said.

We spent a wonderful couple of hours in the big bed in the guest room overlooking the ocean. I didn't even think once about our big new case–the one Ralph hasn't even discussed with us yet.

"You know what we should do now, Bobbie?"

"Go skinny dipping in the pool?"

"My partner always reads my mind. I'd help you out of your clothes, but you're already naked."

"So, let's go!" she said.

The swimming pool was perfectly blocked off from prying eyes on three sides with Leyland cypress trees and had a great view of the ocean on the other. We still had complete privacy because the ocean-facing side was on a bluff. We made love—again—this time in the swimming pool. We both agreed that we need to take more time off from our gruesome tasks of working criminal cases, even though we love our work.

"Hey, Bob, we talked about it the last time we stayed here, so let's put some real planning behind this. Yes, we both love working cases, but isn't it great to get away for a few days? I never had this ocean air in Chicago. Lake Michigan may be pretty, but it doesn't have the wonderful salt-air smell. And the smell of the ocean makes me horny as hell, as you may have noticed."

That night we went to the *Palm East Hampton*, a terrific steakhouse. It was quite expensive, but, with our combined salaries, not to mention my inheritance of $20 million and our book royalty advance of $15 million, we can afford an expensive restaurant, not to mention Hamptons real estate.

CHAPTER THIRTY-FOUR

Bobbie

The following morning, Bob and I made ample use of the excellent gym at our beach house. Working up a sweat does wonders for your brain. Last night Bob and I really worked up some sweat, but not in the gym. Nothing gets my mental faculties flowing better than an evening of sex with Bob. Or an afternoon. Or a morning. Whenever.

CHAPTER THIRTY-FIVE

Bobbie

My cell phone rang, and it was Commissioner Ralph.

"The last time you were there, your vacation was interrupted by a major assignment. Well, this time you won't have a file to work on, because I'm not assigning one to you. I'll save that little surprise for when you return. It will be the biggest case you've ever worked on, perfect for the BBs. Bob, you've been talking about writing another novel, so why not use your time at the beach to work on it? I know Bobbie will love to work on it with you. Relax and enjoy, BBs. You sure as hell deserve it. You guys are due in Washington Friday where you'll appear before Congress for an award."

We looked forward to our award, but we wondered what surprise Ralph had for us.

CHAPTER THIRTY-SIX

Bob

On Friday, Bobbie and I flew to Washington where we were awarded the Congressional Gold Medal. Good grief, the Congressional Gold Medal! Bobbie and I enjoyed another hot shit moment.

When we were awarded our Congressional Gold Medals, Congress was in session. An important budget resolution was up for vote, and the attendance was almost 100 percent. So, we got to bask in applause from the entire House of Representatives. Our medals were draped over our shoulders by Congressman Bob Metcalf, Speaker of the House. I remember his words.

"Bobbie Nelson and Bob Lawton, it's my honor to award you the Congressional Gold Medal, which is bestowed upon those *who have performed an achievement that has an impact on American history and culture that is likely to be recognized as a major achievement in the recipient's field long after the achievement.*"

Bobbie and I know our shit.

With Ralph's okay, we planned to return to our beach house tomorrow.

At 7:30 a.m. on Saturday, Bobbie and I headed for our beach

house in East Hampton. We wanted to get an early start because we love that place. We rented a car from the nearby Hertz outlet. I hate to drive in the city, although I need to in order to get to a crime scene if we can't catch a ride in a patrol car. But this was early morning on a Saturday, so the traffic wasn't bad at all. There will be plenty of traffic as we approach East Hampton, but when we get to the beach house, it will be worth it.

We began our short vacation by walking around the charming village of East Hampton. Bobbie and I are both city people, but we love East Hampton and its calm beauty. At one in the afternoon, we stopped for a light lunch at Bostwick's Chowder House, one of our favorite local eateries. We both had New England clam chowder, which was fabulous.

When we got back to the house, we talked about my upcoming novel. I insisted that it wouldn't be *my* novel, but *ours*. Hell, the last book we collaborated on became a huge best seller, so why go solo now? We envisioned a detective thriller. I want the major protagonist to be a beautiful blond lady named Betty Neilson (Like Bobbie Nelson, get it?). Bobbie insisted that we should have two heroes, Betty Neilson and a handsome guy detective named Rob Layton. "Will there be sex scenes?" I asked.

"Of course, lots of them."

"Will we write them together?"

"Definitely," she said. "How can I write a sex scene without my honey?"

"Okay, I'm in. Rob Layton will be Betty's partner—and lover."

"I think we should have a live rehearsal to get our ideas flowing, baby, sort of like a dry run."

"How dry?"

"Not *too* dry. A shower would be nice. Let's help each other out of our clothes and get on with the rehearsal."

Bobbie kicked off her shoes and unbuckled my belt, all the while staring at me with those gorgeous eyes.

"I think Betty and Rob are in for some excitement, honey. Let's write a few scenes tonight."

"How many scenes?" I asked.

"As many as you can handle, handsome. Now help me out of my panties."

I can feel a best seller in my bones. Well, not just my bones.

CHAPTER THIRTY-SEVEN

Bobbie Nelson

We had another great weekend at our house in East Hampton and returned to Manhattan late on Sunday. At 8:30 on Monday, after we had our usual breakfast at the diner, Bob and I walked into One PP and headed straight for Commissioner Ralph Norquist's office.

He's not only our boss, he's a good friend. He insists we call him Ralph, not Commissioner, although we address him formally when others are around.

Two years ago I was a detective with the Chicago Police Department. At the time, the NYPD was embroiled in a massive scandal of corruption, both on the force and even in the union. On orders from the mayor of New York City, Ralph flew to Chicago to recruit me to join the NYPD as a Detective First Class. After I took him up his offer to visit the NYPD, I accepted the job. I was born and raised in New York City, so the move seemed natural. Also, I love New York. He partnered me with Detective Bob Lawton, who would soon become my lover, my husband, the most important man in my life. I think I fell in love with Bob the day we met, but, cautious that I am, I waited a few weeks before I told him about my feelings. I'll never forget the day I told Bob I loved him. Almost immediately, he told me the same. Our lives had just changed. The BBs were in love!

Bob and I were both dying to talk to Ralph about our beach house in East Hampton, nearby his vacation place, but something about the look on his face told me he had more urgent stuff to talk about. And who was sitting there in front of Ralph but our old friend Buster, Director the CIA, aka Charles Atkins, aka a bunch of other names. He's a Coptic Christian, his parents hailing from Lebanon. He's well known for his ongoing war with radical Islam. "I'm a jihadi's worst nightmare," Buster would say. "I look like them and I talk like them, but I'm not one of them. I hunt them down and kill them." Unlike most CIA directors, Buster came up through the ranks as a field agent. His predecessor referred to Buster as a "super spook" for good reason. Buster is well known as a man who, as he puts it, "takes no shit."

My hunch that Ralph had something urgent to talk about was accurate. Buster stood and gave us both bear hugs. In the time we once spent working as CIA provisional agents we had become good friends.

"I hope you two had a nice time in East Hampton," Ralph said, and immediately changed the subject. "I guess you're wondering why Director Buster is here. We're going to talk about a cluster fuck of Olympian proportions. Over to you, Buster."

"I guess you two have heard about violence on college and university campuses getting out of control," Buster said.

"You're not kidding it's getting out of control," Bobbie said. "You can't turn on the TV without seeing another news report about campus violence."

"I guess you're wondering how this involves me and the CIA," Buster said. "Here's the story in a nutshell. Our people on the ground have found that this shit isn't the normal flareups by some crazy ideologues who are upset about one thing or another. No, it isn't that at all. It's a carefully orchestrated plan and it's coming from the

Middle East, which is why the CIA is involved. Our cyber spies at headquarters have found stuff that will make your heads spin. When you worked with us as a provisional agent at the CIA, Bobbie, you taught us a truckload about designing software algorithms to track fluid data. And what we've found has scared the shit out of us. Here's the bottom line. Some group has a goal to cripple the American higher education system, which is a backbone of our culture and a large part of our economy. The riots we're seeing aren't caused by spontaneous groups of nuts who want to bitch about their latest set of grievances. Somebody is in charge of this shit. Somebody is making it happen."

"Buster, can you give us some numbers so we can appreciate how bad it is," I said.

"As of today, there are 5,300 colleges and universities in the United States, including some small colleges that specialize in one thing or another, up to major institutions like Harvard. Not counting the specialty schools, there has been a full-blown riot at 100 colleges and universities in the past month. That's right, 100 of them. Not a lot of educating is going on. And just like back in the 1960s, a favorite game we see being played is the occupation of a school's administrative offices. The dean's office at Stamford has been occupied for going on three weeks. They, whoever the hell *they* are, also take over the offices of faculty departments. Some parents are yanking their kids out of schools altogether, so as not to waste tuition money on scenes of violence with classes called off. Student loan applications are way off because nobody want to be burdened with a ton of debt and no degree to show for it. At the University of Pennsylvania, not a single class has been conducted in two weeks. Some dedicated professors are inviting students to their homes to conduct classes, but that won't work for large courses. Guys, we're looking at a gigantic economic and cultural war."

"My son is a junior at the University of Michigan," Ralph said.

"He hasn't been to one class in a month. Marlene and I are about to pull him out. As Buster just noted, many people are doing just that. Bob and Bobbie, this is one fucking crisis."

"And how does this involve Bobbie and me?" I figured it was time to ask the obvious question.

"On orders straight from the White House, I'm authorized to deputize you two once again as provisional CIA agents," Buster said. "We need the best detectives in the country on top of this shit, and that, of course, would be you BBs."

"Would that involve Bobbie and I moving to the CIA again?" Bob asked. From the look on his face I could see that he remembered that we looked forward to visiting our beautiful house in East Hampton, not an easy commute from Langley, Virginia.

"No, Bobbie, it won't. You will continue to work out of the NYPD, as Commissioner Ralph will be pleased to know. Your assignment, quite simply, is to quietly infiltrate colleges and universities and gather intelligence. You won't need makeup, but should try to dress like professors, whatever professors dress like these days. Bobbie, you're a friend, and I'm not saying anything out of school when I say that you're a beautiful woman, as your husband Bob knows only too well. Your first job will be to look, how can I say this, 'frumpy.'"

"I hope you don't want me to wear buck teeth like the time when Bob and I were assigned to Chicago to spy on the mob."

Buster and Ralph cracked up. "No, Bobbie, you will still have your lovely smile," Buster said, "But we want you both to look inconspicuous. Nobody is better than you two at getting people to open up and talk. The BBs are the best interrogators on the block. Your jobs are simple: to gather intelligence and find out who the leadership is behind these riots. We've got to find out who or what group is leading this violent movement. It's definitely the leadership we're after. Please try to avoid sounding like cops."

"Buster, my friend," Ralph said, "you're talking to the two best detectives in the country. You don't need to tell these guys how to question people."

I was happy that Ralph reminded Buster of our backgrounds. He's right. Bobbie and I know our shit.

"Where do you recommend that we start?" I asked

"You can pick any college or university, but I recommend NYU. A new president was appointed last week, and he's a great a guy. I've invited him to this meeting, and he'll be here in a few minutes. He isn't your typical university president. He's not afraid to give orders and he expects them to be obeyed. He's a former Marine Corps general."

"What's his name?" I asked.

"Michael Bennett. Most people address him as 'General Mike.' From the look on your face, Bob, it seems like you know him."

"Know him? I served under him as his chief staff officer in Iraq. As you put it, Ralph, he's a great guy. I can't picture him in an academic setting, but General Mike is a flexible leader."

CHAPTER THIRTY-EIGHT

Bobbie

I can't believe we're about to meet Bob's former commanding officer from the Marine Corps. Bob introduced me to him once when the general was in town. Buster said that General Bennett is a big fan of Bob, and I had gotten that same impression when I met the guy. Anybody who's a fan of Bob is a friend of mine.

"General Bennett is here for the meeting, Mr. Commissioner," Ralph's assistant announced.

Although he wore a civilian suit, Bennett looked like a Marine general on a recruiting poster. He's a tall man, at 6'5" and carries himself like the disciplined warrior he once was. He's 58 years old but looks much younger. His short-cropped brown hair was streaked with gray. When he looks at you with his steel blue eyes, you feel compelled to salute.

"Great to see you again, Captain Lawton," Bennett said as he strode over to shake Bob's hand.

"When Commissioner Norquist invited me to this meeting, I was going to call you, Bob, but I figured I'd leave it as a surprise. Hi, Bobbie, good to see you again. I don't know if you folks are aware of this, but Bob Lawton was one of the finest officers in the Marine Corps. One of my proudest moments was when I awarded him the

Bronze Star for valor. Thanks to his quick thinking and heroism, he prevented his rifle company from being overrun. Captain Bob here was one hard-charging grunt."

"Holy shit," I blurted, embarrassing myself.

Bennett resumed speaking, but I couldn't help staring at Bob, *my Bob*, a genuine war hero. What else has he been keeping from me?

"I stand before you folks in a capacity that amazes me, General Mike said. "Never in a million years would I have expected the NYU board of trustees to pick me as president. Military people aren't too popular with university trustees. But with the insanity we've been seeing on campuses across the country, I guess they figured it would be a good idea to pick a president who knows how to give orders. I've spent a lot of time with Director Buster over here, and I've learned that the campus riots we've been seeing are not spontaneous bursts of ideological nonsense, but a concerted effort to undo American higher education. Some group wants to destroy our colleges and universities, and that will be the beginning of an effort to destroy our country. Buster explained what your roles will be, Bob and Bobbie, and I'm here to tell you to consider me part of your team, not just at NYU, but wherever you need me. You served me well in the Marine Corps, Bob, and I'm here to serve you."

"Mr. Commissioner, I suggest you turn on the TV," Ralph's assistant said.

"Good afternoon, ladies and gentlemen, Robin Roberts here for *ABC News*. It seems that every day I bring you yet another report about the violence on American college and university campuses. Today is no different. We are receiving reports that a major riot has broken out at Columbia University, where hundreds of rioters are attacking the school. A large bomb exploded a few minutes ago, destroying the office of Seymour Jenkins, the university president. Fortunately, he was not there at the time, but many of his staff have been killed or injured. As I speak, the fire is raging out of control, and it looks that the entire building may burn to the ground. As with so many of the other incidents, we don't know the pretext for the rioters' actions, other than to maim, kill, and destroy property. The few placards that were caught on videotape read, '*Freedom Now*,' whatever that means. Ladies and gentlemen, America's campuses are being demolished. I will bring you updates on this disturbing story as we get more reports. These aren't just demonstrations, they're riots, they're massive crimes.

"In other news…"

General Bennett continued. "Well, it seems that ABC just gave us a backdrop for this meeting. I'm going to turn this over to Director Buster to fill us in on more information."

"General, if I may…" Buster said.

"Please call me Mike, everybody. As I said, I'm on Bob and Bobbie's team, and we're going to work closely."

"Thanks, General, I mean Mike," Buster said. "Our main job, and Bob and Bobbie will lead the effort, is to gather intelligence. As you've heard, Bob and Bobbie are two sharp-as-hell detectives, and we'll be relying on them heavily. I've spoken often to President Fenton, and although he didn't say it, I think we can assume that we'll declare war on whatever nation is involved in these incidents. Recall the *Bush Doctrine*: Any state that harbors enemy terrorists is itself the enemy. Although it hasn't been formally declared yet, we're at war, a war I intend to win. Mike, would you please review for us your suggested plan?"

"I'm going to give them undercover status and will hire Bob and Bobbie as associate professors of criminology. I know that they both once taught that subject, so it won't take them much to handle the job. I don't suggest they change their names or identities, because they're obviously likely candidates for the jobs. They won't be terribly busy with their teaching schedules because we haven't held a goddam class in any subject for almost a month because of the disturbances. As you know, my main job as a university president is to promote the school and raise money. Well, that's a joke. Since the campus riots began, donations to colleges and universities have slowed to a trickle, which is an obvious aim of whoever is behind this shit. I'll have plenty of time to help Bob and Bobbie in their intelligence gathering. I must run along. I just got a text from my assistant that a large mob is forming at NYU. We have some interesting times ahead of us."

We'd soon find out just how interesting those times will be.

CHAPTER THIRTY-NINE

Bob

After we met with the Commissioner, Bobbie and I went to our office.

"Hey, handsome, I need to tell you how proud I am of you. Oh my God, the Bronze Star. I had read about it when I researched you, but I didn't delve into detail because I'm not really up on military stuff and I had no idea that the Bronze Star was for heroism. From what General Mike said, you saved the lives of your entire rifle company. My honey is a real war hero."

"Forget about being proud. Just tell me you love me—that's my highest award."

"Yes, I love you, baby, and I'm also proud of you. I knew I married a great guy, but now I'm finding out that I married a *great man*. You're the best, honey. I think it's fabulous that we'll be working with General Mike, your old boss."

"I agree. I could see that Mike is treating this operation as a mission, and having served under him in Iraq, I can tell you that General Mike likes successful missions. So, what do you think, Bobbie, how do you see us working this program?"

"Basic detective work, hon. I see us quietly working the crowds and asking questions without looking like cops. That's something you and I know how to do better than anybody. Hey, *Detectiving* is in our blood. I think we should use voice recorders. If we're seen jotting things down into our notebooks it would look suspicious, although I hate the idea of not using my notebook. I think we should drop hints to start conversations. Something tells me that the average demonstrator is not part of the management behind this crap, and they'll give a spontaneous reaction to whatever we say."

"Hey, we should go shopping and buy some professorial-looking clothes."

"What do you think of Buster's idea that I should look *frumpy*, Bob?"

"You can't do the impossible, Bobbie, and for you to look frumpy is just that, impossible. You're breathtakingly beautiful. But you should get some baggy clothes, so the bastards don't get distracted by your gorgeous figure."

"So where should we start, honey?"

"Where we always start—*together.*"

CHAPTER FORTY

Bobbie

Bob and I reported to the pre-law department on a Wednesday morning at the Greenwich Village campus of NYU. The old uptown campus at University Heights in the Bronx is a thing of the past, having closed in 1973 because of financial problems. The old uptown campus now houses Bronx Community College. The pre-law department at the Greenwich Village campus includes the subject of criminology, the course that Bob and I will teach.

The campus was somewhat quiet that day, except for about 50 students gathered in Washington Square Park with placards saying, "Fuck You NYU." At least they're articulate.

We each carried a bag loaded with books, trying to look as faculty-like as possible. I wore a pair of baggy jeans and a light denim jacket. I don't know if I looked *frumpy* as Buster suggested, but I sure as hell felt like it.

"Hey, Professor Frump. No matter how you're dressed, I get horny as jackrabbit just looking at you."

Bob is so sweet and loves to throw flattery my way. God, do I love this man.

Bob and I had started to take Arabic lessons with an online

Rosetta Stone course, and It wasn't easy. Even though I'm pretty good at languages, I was having a hard time with Arabic. It bears little similarity to any of the tongues I speak. Our main objective was to catch snippets of conversations. Then we'd try to make sense of those snippets.

Bob and I casually walked past a few of the placard carriers. We're good at appearing "casual." Because we've worked undercover so many times, it just comes naturally. I overheard a guy saying in Arabic, "Stern at 1 p.m.," apparently referring to the Stern School of Business. I *think* that's what he said, but he could have said, "What's for lunch?" My Arabic definitely needs work.

On the hunch that I got it right, Bob and I walked in front of the Stern School of Business at 1 p.m. I *did* get it right, I was pleased to see. All 50 of the placard people marched up to the entrance, this time chanting the words on their placards, "Fuck You NYU," a five-syllable phrase perfect for a chant. I wondered if they're good at poetry.

As Bob and I strolled through the entrance, one of the placard boys ran after us. The son of a bitch grabbed my jacket from behind, almost dumping me on my ass. Bob hauled back and delivered a right hook to the creep's jaw. From the cracking sound I was sure he broke it. It's a bad idea to mess with Marine Captain Bob. We continued on our way to the auditorium, where we assumed a demonstration would be held. I glanced over my shoulder and saw Mr. Broken Jaw try to communicate with one of his colleagues. He was hardly able to speak. Bob throws a wicked punch.

We sat at the rear of the auditorium. One of the placard folks sat next to me. "Are you guys from the ACLU?" I asked. The guy answered me in pigeon Arabic. It was obvious he couldn't speak a word of English. Curious, because all the classes are taught in English. Obviously, this guy was off-campus talent. No way in hell was he an American university student. I whispered a note into my recording device.

Another placard guy sat in front of us. "Do you think we should leave?" Bob said, a simple non-suspicion-arousing question, one aimed at starting a conversation. Bob is cool. The guy turned his head and said, in perfect English, "Why miss the fun?"

Within a minute, four of the placard boys ran to the head of the auditorium with some sort of tanks strapped to their backs. They hosed down the auditorium platform with whatever was in the tanks. One of the guys slipped and fell on his ass. Obviously, the tanks contained some sort of oily substance. Another one of the placard people threw a lit cigarette lighter to the stage, which quickly became engulfed in flames. Holy shit, they're burning the building down.

"Let's go," Bob said.

We walked quickly out of the soon-to-be-burning building, surrounded by placard bearers. I ducked into an alcove and dialed 911 to report the fire.

When we got outside, Bob and I typed into our cellphones, or made it appear so. Actually, we were taking photos of the placard folks as they emerged from the building. I also listened carefully with my newfound, although slight, understanding of Arabic. I repeatedly heard the word "brotherhood,' sometimes in English. Phrases like "The Brotherhood strikes again" were repeated over and over, along with the familiar, "Alahu Akbar" (*God is the greatest*).

I heard one guy, an apparent leader judging from his position in the crowd, say to another man named Mustaffa, "I just reported our glory to Sana'a." He said it in English. Oh, my God. Could this be pay dirt? Sana'a is the capital of Yemen, although there is some dispute about that. According to Buster, Yemen is a "cesspool of terrorism." I whispered what I had just heard to Bob. He stared at me wide-eyed and dictated a note into his device.

The placard folks appeared excited as they watched the Stern School of Business go up in flames. Although we hated to see the destruction of university property, we both realized that excitement is good for an investigation, because excitement often results in loose lips. We both realized that taking photos was important, because many of the faces will eventually be hooked up with names by our facial recognition department. I heard constant references to Sana'a and the brotherhood as we clicked photos of the speakers. It was as if they were all writing lyrics to the same song.

We stopped by the office of General Mike to report what we saw. He was distracted, to say the least, as one of his major buildings—the Stern School of Business—burned to the ground. Obviously, Mike didn't have the time for a meeting. I guess General Mike figured his new role as a university president would be much more peaceful than commanding a Marine regiment in a war zone. Doesn't seem to be working out that way.

"I'll call you as soon as I can get a couple of minutes," General Mike said. "I want to hear what you've heard."

We realized that we had gathered enough evidence for one day and wanted to get back to the office to compare notes and make phone calls. One of the calls would be to our friend Rick Bellamy, Secretary of Homeland Security, who owns a brownstone near the NYU campus. We wanted to let him know that his home is right near ground zero, a scene of horrible violence. An unmarked car picked us up near the entrance to Washington Square Park. I noticed that the chant began again, "Fuck You NYU." I also noticed that they chanted with Middle Eastern accents. As I watched the smoke billowing from the remains of the Stern School of Business, I realized that this was not the typical detective assignment for Bob and me. We told the driver to take us to the back of One Police Plaza, not the main entrance. Our new assignment required a lot of secrecy.

We'd soon find out that a lot of secrets were being kept from us.

CHAPTER FORTY-ONE

Bob

W e went straight to Ralph Norquist's office to report the day's findings. Buster had already returned to Langley. We told Ralph what we found, but especially what Bobbie heard with her improving Arabic ear.

"So, you heard Sana'a, the capital of Yemen, repeated as well as the word 'brotherhood.' Did you hear anything about ISIS or al Qaeda?"

"No, not one mention of those words," Bobbie said, "but this was only our first day. Bob and I took dozens of photos, which we'll give to the facial recognition people right now."

"I suggest you call Phil Cummings in California, a CIA agent staking out Stanford University. Phil is fluent in Arabic and you can compare notes with him."

"My Arabic definitely needs work, Ralph. Yes, I picked up a few things, but not nearly as many as I missed."

We then went to the office where the facial recognition technicians do their stuff and gave them all the photos we took that day. Bobbie's Arabic may need work, but as detectives we know what we're doing.

Bobbie then placed a call to CIA Agent Phil Cummings on Ralph's suggestion. If our observations are similar, we thought, we may be close to zeroing in on the case.

It didn't happen that way.

Cummings, who had been staking out Stanford University, had a shock for us. He told us he didn't hear the word 'Sana'a' nor the word 'brotherhood' at all, not even once. And he had been on his stakeout for five days. He did hear a lot of references to Riyadh, the capital of Saudi Arabia, and one reference to ISIS. He also heard a lot of references to Tehran. Tehran? Shit, our stakeouts aren't showing any similarities. "Back to the drawing board" is a phrase that all detectives hate, but that's exactly where we found ourselves, back to the fucking drawing board. But then it occurred to me that the dissimilarities between what Cummings heard and what I heard may be clues in themselves. Detective work means keeping open to possibilities.

With the burning down of the Stern School of Business, we figured the NYU campus would be relatively free of protesters and rioters, at least for a few days. So, tomorrow we would visit Fordham University in the Bronx. According to our data, Fordham has seen its share of radical activity in the past few weeks.

We called General Mike to update him on our activities.

"Captain Bob," General Mike said, "I wish to hell I had a rifle company under my command with you leading it. I cannot fucking believe that the Stern School of Business has burned to the ground. It looks like my new job is burning out from under me. We've got a goddam war on our hands, folks. I can't believe I'm saying this, but NYU reminds me of Iraq. I'll see you guys in a few days."

Because we weren't listed on the faculty at Fordham, we would need to wear elaborate disguises, something to which Bobbie and I had grown accustomed. No padding, no buck teeth, but disguises nonetheless. We would both wear the uniforms of United Maintenance

Company. Commissioner Ralph ordered them delivered to our apartment, where we tried them on.

"My, you look charmingly frumpy in your maintenance uniform, Bobbie."

"At least I'm not wearing buck teeth, wiseass. Hey, let's have a martini, honey. Something tells me that Fordham will be quite interesting tomorrow."

CHAPTER FORTY-TWO

Bobbie

I hate disguises, but sometimes they're necessary. Bob and I couldn't risk being recognized by one of the placard people at Fordham who may have seen us at NYU. Buster had told us that the demonstrators often move from one campus to another. I recalled our covers being blown when we spied on the mob in Chicago. That little adventure almost got me killed. Needless to say, Bob and I didn't want that to happen again.

Also, we didn't have the cover of being faculty members as we did at NYU, so our Fordham persona would need to be different. I must say I looked lovely in my baggy United Maintenance Company overalls. My floppy baseball cap also looked charming.

We walked into the student union building and tried to look busy as maintenance workers. We moved light folding chairs from one wall to another, hoping that nobody would realize that what we were doing made no sense at all. Our strategy today would be walk around and start conversations, something Bob and I are good at.

Holding one of the chairs, I walked over to a young woman who was reading a magazine. In my years as a detective, I've developed a sixth sense for talking to people who seem communicative. Bob has the same talent. "Wow, these campus riots are sure getting out of hand, aren't they?" I said. "Did you hear about that building being burned down at NYU yesterday?"

"Yes, I did, but it hasn't happened here at Fordham—yet."

I introduced myself, and she told me her name was Dolores. I told her my name was Roberta.

Well, it is, although nobody has called me that since I was a kid.

She seemed to want to talk. "The semester ends next week and I'm out of here. My parents refuse to pay any more tuition to a place where classes are regularly cancelled because some pack of assholes are protesting something. I don't blame them. I can't afford to pay my own tuition, so it looks like I won't be getting a university degree anytime soon."

What Dolores just told me was something I'd heard with gut-wrenching regularity—kids dropping out of school.

"Do you have any idea who is behind this crap?" I asked, walking into the opening she just created.

"You haven't heard?" Dolores said. "It's an outfit called EOA. I'm told it means '*End of America*.' At first, I thought it was bullshit, because it sounded so dramatic, but I've been told that by so many people I'm beginning to believe it."

Holy shit, this may be an important lead. My recording device in the pocket of my United Maintenance Company overalls was doing its thing.

"Do you have any idea where that organization is located, Dolores?"

"Somewhere in the Middle East, from what I've heard."

"You don't speak Arabic by any chance, do you, Dolores?" Hey, sometimes grabbing for a straw in the wind pays off.

"No, I don't but my roommate does." Dolores then told me the Arabic words for *End of America* or EOA. I dictated the information into my recording device.

Oh my God. I recalled that I heard that phrase countless times yesterday at NYU, although I didn't understand it at the time.

Dolores excused herself and got up to leave.

"Running to class?" I asked.

"I wish. I have a dentist appointment. Nice talking to you, Roberta."

A dentist appointment rather than a class, just another symptom of the crazy shit we were going through.

Bob and I decided to have lunch at the cafeteria in the student union building. Just a couple of maintenance workers taking a break.

"I noticed you talking to that guy wearing a hat, Bob. Did he have anything interesting to say?"

"Yeah, I'll say it was interesting. Ever hear the phrase '*End of America*?' It seems like a major clue."

"I just heard it from that girl I was talking to. She even gave me the Arabic translation of the phrase. I realized I heard it constantly yesterday at NYU. After lunch, let's do a little more furniture moving and then head back to One PP and work the phones."

CHAPTER FORTY-THREE

So how was your day, honey?" Nancy Drummond said to her husband. Carl Drummond was the Dean of Academic Affairs at the University of Iowa. She laughed as she said it.

"I'm glad to see you laughing when you asked me that question. To answer you, my day sucked, as does every day on my job. Once again, the executive committee of the board told me to cancel all classes. This has been going on for three weeks. What am I running, a chat room?"

"Hey, Carl, when I asked you how your day was, I was making a joke. But I notice you aren't laughing."

"How can I laugh? The demonstrators are once again taking over the goddam university. And now I'm worried about something else—my job. Why the hell do they need an academic dean if there's no academics going on? All I do is sit in my office answering emails, browsing the Web, and reading books. Sometimes, to make my day a bit more interesting, I listen to an audiobook."

"Is there anything new, or is it just more of the same?" Nancy said.

"Yes, there is something new. The demonstrations, to use a ridiculous term, are becoming increasingly violent. That shocked me—at first. Everybody knows that the school is covered by surveillance cameras, and you know that if cameras are trained on you, you will eventually be arrested if you're caught engaging in violence. But no arrests have been made. I spoke to the local police chief, and he had some interesting observations. He told me that they tried everything they could to track down the violent demonstrators, but they weren't able to find anybody. You heard me; the bastards who were caught on camera can't be found. There seems to be steady waves of new demonstrators every week, replacing the ones our surveillance cameras picked up. You know me well, Nancy, and you know that I've been a supporter of academic freedom all my life, and yes, sometimes that freedom includes demonstrations. But these aren't demonstrations, they're fucking riots. We've been trying to get a handle on just what the demonstrations are aimed at. That got us nowhere. The demonstrations seem to have one simple objective—to shut down the university. If this crap continues nationwide, we'll be looking at our country being shut down. I just hope the government gets off its ass and does something about this."

CHAPTER FORTY-FOUR

Bob

Yesterday, Bobbie and I had a few more chats with students as we moved folding chairs from one wall to another. I wonder if anybody noticed our pointless furniture moving. We again heard the words *End of America* and the acronym, EOA, and also heard that the people we spoke to think that the organization, if you can call it that, is from the Middle East. Outside the student union building we heard a chant starting up. *End of America* seemed to be the words of choice among the chanters. Guess it beats, *Fuck You NYU,* especially because we were at Fordham.

When we walked into Ralph Norquist's office, none other than CIA Director Buster was there. As long as I've known him, I've noticed that Buster has a knack for showing up unannounced out of nowhere. We were happy to see him and looked forward to one of his detailed updates.

"Agent Phil Cummings reported to me from Stanford," Buster said. "He's heard the words *End of America* and EOA constantly. He thinks the words are new, because he just began hearing them. But now he hears them non-stop. My IT guys have inserted the words into their search algorithm. I wish Bobbie Nelson was there to help us."

Bobbie just smiled. She's grown accustomed to Buster's flattery of her skills.

"We don't know if it's the name of an organization or just a phrase some group likes to use, such as the Iranian epithet of choice, *Death to America,*" Buster said, "but it does give us something to focus on. And we sure as hell need something to focus on. Phil Cummings confirmed that he's also heard that the people saying the words come from somewhere in the Middle East. Let me tell you about some news I got from the Department of Education. College and university applications have slowed to a trickle, and dropouts are sprouting like bamboo. People are looking at American institutions of higher learning as the equivalent of walking into a riot, which isn't far from accurate."

Buster's assistant walked in—she didn't even knock as she grabbed the remote and turned on the TV. "Check this out, guys."

"Bill Hemmer for *Fox News* ladies and gentlemen. The unrest on American college campuses can no longer just be thought of as unrest, but full-blown criminal violence. Yesterday at the University of Wisconsin, a building was bombed. It burned to the ground before emergency vehicles arrived at the scene. This same thing happened a week ago at Columbia and two days ago at NYU. At the University of Delaware just this morning, there was a full-scale riot, accompanied by gunfire. You heard me—gunfire. Here in New York City, the president's office at Hunter College has been occupied by 30 armed protesters. *Fox News* management has assigned a full-time producer and five reporters to cover the campus violence. If you wish to avoid danger, one way to accomplish that is by avoiding college campuses. Of course, that begs the question: Where do the students go? Needless to say, *Fox News* will be following this story closely and constantly. In other news…"

"I imagine you're flooding the Middle East with operatives, Buster," Bobbie said.

"I can't confirm that."

"You just did," she said, laughing. Buster has discovered over time that he can't bullshit Bobbie.

Buster cracked up.

"One thing that amazes me," I said, "is the number of demonstrators and rioters across the country. How the hell do they recruit all these people?"

"From the accents we're hearing," Buster said, "we think most come from Middle Eastern countries. Besides that, there are people in our country who just love to protest—anything, whether they understand it or not. But they have *leadership* and that's what we need to learn about. There's nothing spontaneous about this violence. They make the 1960s look like nothing more than Beatles music. So, it's the management we're after, the group that is organizing this violence and making it happen. Soon, our moles on the ground will tell us more."

He looked at Bobbie and winked when he said that. Although he wouldn't admit to flooding the Middle East with operatives because Bobbie and I don't have the sacred "need to know," it was obvious that the CIA is doing just that. Having worked with Buster before, we know that he plays rough—*very rough*. Whenever Buster says that his people have had a "talk" with someone, we know what it means—The person being talked to has just returned to room temperature.

"We're inviting some suspected terrorists to come to Langley to be interrogated."

"Inviting them?" Bobbie said.

"Yes, at the CIA we're very polite. Which brings me to a request I want to make of Commissioner Ralph here. When we have a few 'guests' in place I want the two best interrogators in the land to help us. That, of course, would be the BBs."

Bobbie and I are scheduled to spend a few days at our new waterfront home the day after tomorrow. I wondered if we'll ever get to visit the Hamptons.

"Consider it done, Buster," Commissioner Ralph said. "Bob and Bobbie will join you at the CIA. I'll repeat what you've heard me say often—please don't steal my best detectives away from me. Just let us know when you have enough 'guests' for them to interrogate."

CHAPTER FORTY-FIVE

Bobbie

O ur new assignment, especially now that we'll be headed often to Langley, won't allow for much time off. Maybe we can watch videos about waterfront homes.

Bob and I are scheduled to fly to Langley tomorrow to interrogate Buster's "guests."

Our plane touched down at Dulles Airport at 10:30 a.m. A CIA car awaited us to bring us to Langley. We met with Buster in his office, where he introduced us to Marcia Barrett, an agent who was fluent in Arabic and Farsi. My studies have been coming along, and so have Bob's, but with something as important as an interrogation we knew we'd need a translator. The three of us walked to the interrogation room, which was equipped with the usual one-way mirror. The room was pleasantly cool at 72 degrees, which was good, because Bob and I would soon be turning up the heat.

Mustaffa Antar was a skinny guy, about age 30, with a long beard and a shock of black hair. I immediately disliked the guy, especially because he and his colleagues were keeping Bob and me from our beautiful new vacation home in East Hampton. But we have an important interrogation in front of us, so I tamped down my negative emotions as I always do. To be a good interrogator it's essential to keep your emotions under tight control, so I ignored my desire to punch this creep in the nose. His English was pretty good, so Marcia would be needed only for the occasional word or phrase.

Bob and I agreed that he'd begin the questioning, in case Mustaffa had an issue with being questioned by a woman. If he does, fuck him. I'll be all over his head in a few minutes.

After some preliminary chitchat, Bob got down to business.

"Mr. Antar, are you familiar with the words *End of America*, also stated as EOA?"

"I am not knowings what you be speaking about."

Marcia, a tall pretty brunette, is well known in the agency as a "tough broad," one who doesn't put up with shit from an interrogee.

She spoke to him in English, more like yelled at him. "Mr. Antar, you are aware that the CIA has guaranteed you leniency in exchange for your full cooperation. Unless you want your sorry ass in prison for the rest of your life, I suggest being straightforward with us. And I know that you can speak perfect English, so stop playing fucking games and answer Detective Lawton's question."

I was happy that Marcia was there. She'd make a good cop.

"I repeat my question," Bob said, "are you familiar with the words *End of America*, also stated as EOA?"

"Yes," Mustaffa said, staring at the floor.

"Is it an organization?" Bob asked. "Hey, look at me and answer my question, please."

"It's sort of an organization."

"Like you're *sort of* an asshole?" Marcia inquired. I really was getting to like this lady.

"It's more like a movement," Mustaffa said.

"So, *End of America* is a movement?" I said. "Please tell us the names of the people who run this movement." Bob had nodded to me, indicating that I should join in the questioning.

"There is only one person. His name is Randolfo Martin."

Bob, Marcia, and I just stared. We couldn't believe what we had just heard.

"Oh, dear God," I said. "Oh, dear God Almighty."

Randolfo Martin is the son of the late Bartholomew Martin, the former President of the United States, America's first and only dictator. Bartholomew Martin defeated Matt Blake after he waged a campaign of lies and slander, portraying Blake as being soft on terrorism. The day before the election saw horrible scenes of explosions at children's amusement parks around the country. The Bartholomew Martin people, with their billions in bribe money, convinced journalists that the explosions were the result of Matt Blake's actions or inactions. A subsequent investigation found that the bombings were caused by Martin's people, although it couldn't be proven. Martin won in a landslide, and he brought with him a veto-proof majority in both houses of Congress. Overnight, we Americans saw our basic rights evaporate in a storm of executive orders, affirmed by a compliant Congress. Within a few months we barely recognized our country. The cradle of liberty had become a cradle of executive orders. Blake defeated him in the next election, thank God. The American voters had become fed up with our liberties being stolen. Three years later Martin was accused of bombing the Republican National Convention where Harry Fenton had just won the nomination for the next presidential election. Martin was arrested, tried, and convicted of 412 counts of first-degree murder. A lot of Americans, myself included, felt relieved when he was assassinated in prison. His older son, Antonio Martin is serving a life sentence in prison. When Antonio Martin was the president of the rogue nation, Concordia, he aimed his sights on the world's shipping industry, and almost brought it to a halt. Dozens of ships were sent to the bottom of the sea, along with passengers and crews. Lovely family.

Buster has told me that he thinks Randolfo, age 41, may be the worst of the Martins. Buster calls him a "ruthless scumbag." He has been hiding in the shadows, typical of a Martin, quietly planning the latest surprise for the United States. And now our interrogee tells us that Randolfo is behind the campus riots and heads up the "movement" called the *End of America*. We suddenly had a new ballgame—and a new opponent.

"And where is Randolfo Martin located?" I asked, when I recovered my voice.

"I can't say."

"Horseshit," Marcia yelled, "where is the man located?" Marcia was definitely becoming my favorite spook.

"Tehran," Mustaffa said.

"Bob, we need to take a short break," I said. "Buster needs to hear this."

Marcia speed-dialed Buster on her phone. He walked into the interrogation room in less than three minutes, while an agent escorted our interrogee to the hallway.

"We have two words for you, Buster," I said. "Randolfo Martin."

Like the seasoned spy he is, Buster is talented at putting on a poker face. He disciplines himself to hide his feelings from the person he was speaking to, so he could keep his thoughts to himself. But he didn't even try to mask his feelings. He stared at us wide-eyed and took a deep breath, exhaling audibly.

"Oh, my God, Randolfo Martin," Buster said. "We've been trying to keep track of him, but he just disappeared. Did you find out where he is?"

"Tehran," Bob said. "Our interrogee didn't want to disclose that, but your colleague Marcia here is quite a persuasive woman."

"I've told anyone who would listen, including President Fenton, that Randolfo is the worst of the evil Martin family," Buster said. "The son of a bitch will stop at nothing to amass power, and now he wants to destroy America's higher education system. He may be holed up in Tehran, but we can be sure he has thousands of his followers across the United States."

Marcia's cellphone sounded with a chime.

"I think we should turn on the TV, Buster." He insists that everybody, including subordinates, simply call him Buster.

"Norah O'Donnell for *CBS News*, ladies and gentlemen. We have yet another sickening story of campus violence to report. An estimated 200 protesters have invaded the administration building at Brown University in Providence, Rhode Island. I call them protesters, but, as usual, it's unclear just what they're protesting. Besides screaming, shouting, and chanting profanities, this event involved hundreds of rocks thrown at every window. This comes on the heels of another riot three hours ago at the University of New Mexico, where hundreds of rioters also threw stones. Besides millions of dollars in property damage, these events hit right at the core of what these schools are all about—teaching students. In campus after campus, these riots are resulting in regular classes being cancelled. It's no exaggeration to say that our nation's higher educational system is under a massive attack. We will be following these stories closely, so stay tuned to *CBS News* for the latest."

"I've got to take this to the White House," Buster said. "Something tells me that President Fenton will want to take the gloves off."

CHAPTER FORTY-SIX

Randolfo Martin met with his aide William Tomlinson on the deck of his palatial mansion in Tehran, overlooking two acres of manicured gardens. A koi pond was placed right next to the deck. They sat on chairs on the mahogany deck with a view of the beautiful gardens. Tall grasses swayed in the gentle breeze as the koi nibbled at the water's surface, begging for tasty treats. A 12-gauge shotgun was nestled next to Martin's chair.

"Tell me, William, what do you have to report on our latest attacks?"

"I have excellent news, sir…"

"Sir? How many times do I have to tell you, William, that my name is Randolfo, not sir or any other name you choose for me? And don't tell me you have *excellent* news. Just give me the facts and I'll do the evaluating."

Like his father and brother before him, Randolfo insists on a strict set of communication rules. He always referred to a subordinate by his full first name. William was William, never Bill or Will. He also insists that subordinates call him by his full first name. And he also demands that an aide never give him adjectives or adverbs when describing something. He wants to do his own analyzing, not as handed to him by a bootlicking subordinate looking to impress his superior.

"Our 'demonstrations' are having their desired effect, Randolfo. In the past week alone, we have seen riots at no fewer than 50 American colleges and universities. As you planned, the riots are resulting in massive cancellation of classes. As soon as a class is announced, we launch another demonstration. As you know, sir, I mean Randolfo, we have been concentrating on large colleges and universities. Soon we will train our sites on smaller institutions and junior colleges as you have commanded. According to a report by the American Treasury Secretary, property damage alone has passed the $500 million mark. You picked the appropriate name for this movement, *End of America*, because that is what we are seeing."

"What, if anything, is being done to combat us, William?"

"On-campus security guards as well as local police forces have tried to stop our efforts, but they are overwhelmed by the number of people we throw into the demonstrations. That famous detective couple, Bobbie Nelson and Bob Lawton, known as the BBs, are spearheading the effort. Although they are detectives with the NYPD, they have been deputized as CIA provisional agents. I expect those two to give us a lot of problems. But, as you know, our people are well disciplined. They move from campus to campus to avoid their photos being taken by surveillance cameras. They're not only well disciplined, but they also carefully coordinate their activities."

"That is all, William. I expect another full report in two days."

Randolfo lit a cigar as he looked out over the gardens and laughed. "Yes, the *End of America* is coming."

CHAPTER FORTY-SEVEN

Bob

S addle up, honey, we're going to the Oval Office," I said.

"Are you serious?"

"I just got off the phone with Buster. President Fenton wants to meet with us as well as Buster and General Mike from NYU. Mike is in Washington today and he'll meet us there."

"Why would the President want to meet with us and General Mike?" Bobbie asked.

"I have no idea, but I'm sure it's important."

A CIA car picked up Bobbie, Buster, and me at Reagan Airport for the 30-minute drive to the White House. We had just heard about another campus riot, this one at the University of Vermont. The office of the school's president is occupied by at least 25 people. All classes, of course, have been cancelled. This shit was no longer starting to get out of control. It *was* out of control.

Two Marine guards met us under the porte cochere leading into the West Wing. The Marines, I noticed, weren't just wearing side arms but had M16 rifles slung over their shoulders.

When we entered the Oval Office, General Mike was already

there, as well as First Lady, Meg. President Fenton, always the gentleman, stood to greet us. A former five-star admiral, the President always carries himself with a military bearing. He didn't look happy. First Lady, Meg, who I always think is almost as beautiful as Bobbie (almost), looked tired, not her usual effusive self.

"I'm about to do something I hate, but I have little choice," President Fenton said. "I'm suspending the Posse Comitatus Act of 1878, and I'm declaring a countrywide emergency under the National Emergencies Act of 1976. The Posse Comitatus Act, as you know, precludes members of the armed forces from acting in a civilian setting. But the police departments across the country simply don't have enough personnel to combat these goddam campus riots. I've asked my old friend General Mike Bennett here to join us today. Mike, when you were hired as President of NYU, I figure you thought you'd have a nice quiet job after your courageous service in the Marines. Looks like you're back in combat, except without a uniform and a weapon."

"I'm honored to be here, Mr. President. As you know I was once the commanding officer of Bob Layton here. Captain Bob was the finest officer in my command. He's a great guy."

"He's the best," Bobbie said, smiling. Damn, she can be embarrassing at times.

"The reason I invited Bob and Bobbie to be with us today is because they're two of the sharpest detectives in any police department, if not *the* sharpest. It should come as no surprise that Bob and Bobbie, with their amazing skills at interrogation, have discovered that none other than Randolfo Martin is our enemy."

"The most miserable scumbag on earth," the First Lady said.

"I think The First Lady characterizes him accurately, if somewhat bluntly. Like his father Bartholomew and his brother Antonio before him, Randolfo Martin is one of the most dedicated enemies our country has ever faced. With his hordes of adoring minions, he is attacking the heart of America, our higher education system. According to the Secretary of Education, there hasn't been a regularly scheduled class at most colleges or universities in seven days, and at some institutions it's been over a month. The University of Vermont cancelled its classes this morning after the president's office was forcibly occupied. That Randolfo Martin bastard is holding the nation's youth hostage to his insane delusions. And he's picked the safest place he could find to hide, Iran, a country that means us nothing but harm, a country only too happy to host our enemy. I just may need to ask Congress to declare war on Iran. I believe in what's been called *The Bush Doctrine*, after President George W. Bush—a country that harbors our enemy *is* our enemy. War is a bad thing, but that's what is going on, a war. As I found out in my many years at sea, sometimes the pathway to peace is covered with violence. Director Buster, do you have any comments?"

Buster got visibly pale because he needed to be careful with his words.

"Intelligence gathering is the most important thing, sir, and that's why I'm happy to have a couple of outstanding New York City cops working with us. Bob and Bobbie have taught us a few things at Langley about computer algorithms, not to mention the fine art of interrogating suspects."

"Buster, I know that you're fanatical, to use a word, about the 'need to know.' Do you think you can share with these folks the intelligence you've gathered about the identities of the rioters?"

Buster wiped some perspiration from his forehead.

"Yes, sir, I can share that, because it's not something we're keeping secret. Thanks to intelligence from Bob and Bobbie here, as well as our agents on stakeout at other colleges and universities across the country, it almost seems like a foreign army is occupying our campuses. From the photographs they've given us, we see a lot of people on the CIA and FBI watch lists—a *lot*. We know that these 'protesters' as they call themselves, aren't your typical fanatics looking to raise hell about perceived injustices. The world of journalism seems to have gotten the message too. From what we've learned from just Bob and Bobbie alone, a large number of the campus radicals don't even speak English, not a word of it."

"General Mike, do you want to say something?" the President said.

"Yes, sir, to amplify what Buster just said, we've been seeing these events play out at NYU as well. And if I may comment on your intention to use the armed forces, I must agree, although it isn't my place to agree or not. I hate the idea as much as you, sir, but the only alternative is to simply cede control of our country's campuses to the foreign radicals. We find ourselves in a defensive posture, and that's what we need to do—to defend our institutions of higher learning."

"Which brings me to another announcement I want to make," the President said. "Mike, as a university president and former Marine general, you have some unique qualifications. I want to appoint you to a new position in our government, Director of Campus Security. Besides your reputation as a warrior, I also know that you're an impeccable administrator. Our defensive forces on campuses will be coordinated through your office. It will be part of the Department of Homeland Security, and you will work closely with Secretary Rick Bellamy, a terrific guy. You'll be stationed at the New York office at Federal Plaza, with plenty of support from the FBI, not to mention Bob and Bobbie and the NYPD as needed. But you'll need to resign your position as president of New York University. Does that work for you, Mike?"

"I'll be honored to take the position, Mr. President, and I have no problem resigning from NYU. As a university president my major job is public relations and fundraising. Raising money in this environment is almost impossible. My chief of staff told me that she finds it difficult to even book me for a speaking engagement. I also look forward to working with Detectives Bob and Bobbie. Nobody is better than them at working tough cases. And the word *tough* barely describes what we're faced with. We'll get this done, Mr. President."

As we drove back to the CIA, Buster said, "No sense you guys sticking around indefinitely at the CIA. You can fly down here if you're needed to supervise some interrogations, but you're free to head back home to the NYPD. I know Commissioner Norquist will be delighted to hear that."

So, Bobbie and I headed back to the NYPD. Our lives have taken a weird turn of late. We stared into each other's eyes. Whatever shit life throws my way, at least I have Bobbie at my side.

CHAPTER FORTY-EIGHT

Bobbie

Our flight from Washington landed at JFK at 9:30 a.m. on Friday.

"Hey, Bob, do you know what this is?" I said, as we climbed into our Uber.

"Well, it appears to be a laptop computer."

"It certainly is, and it works as well in East Hampton as it does here. Let's take off for a few days and head for our beautiful waterfront home."

Bob didn't say anything. He wrapped his arms around me and kissed me on the lips, a deep, hot, hungry kiss. I think he liked my idea.

I called the Commissioner's office to let him know we'd be taking off for a few days.

"Great," Ralph said. "Marlene and I are headed to our place in about an hour. We're dying to see your new house. Let's plan on dinner tonight."

Bob and I pulled up to our beautiful East Hampton house at 1:15 p.m. It was mid-June, and the weather was perfect, with low humidity and temperatures in the mid-70s. The house looked even better than the first time we saw it. We carried some luggage with us so we could outfit the house for our brief stays. I hoped the stays wouldn't be too infrequent. Our lives recently had been nonstop stress, and we agreed that buying this place was one of our better ideas. Bob and I would never be completely off the job, but with a beautiful office overlooking Georgica Pond, we could get work done and relax at the same time. A laptop, a cellphone, and an Internet hookup and we're ready to boogie. An IT crew has already set up heavy-duty encryption protocols for everything on our Web connection. We walked around the gigantic house and reacquainted ourselves with it. When we walked into the game room, Bob challenged me to a game of pool. I always loved to play pool and would do so often in Chicago with my pal, Janice Patton. I must admit that I'm pretty good at billiards, although I hadn't played it in a while.

"You like to shoot pool?" Bob said, with a look of happy shock on his face.

"I don't like it, I *love* it. Rack 'em up, baby."

Bob's a very good pool player—and so am I. We flipped a coin to see who would go first, and I won. We agreed that we'd play three games. Bob laughed when I *ran the table* on my first round, sinking every ball, winning the game. Then he did the same. No surprise—we are always discovering new things about each other. Bob won the three-game match by two points, and I took my clothes off. Yes, I took my clothes off—that was our wager. I know, I know, we're crazy. Strip billiards? Don't knock it if you haven't tried it.

Bob took me by the hand and led me to our bedroom. I was already naked, so I helped Bob out of his clothes. As I slid down his underpants I looked down. I could see that he was just as excited as me. We wrapped our arms around each other and made out, naked, as if it was our first time. If there's one positive thing about stress, it's what you do to relieve it. And we did just that. We climbed into bed and I held his beautiful erection in both hands. I kissed him on his gorgeous lips, then his chest, then worked my way down to the happy zone. Bob groaned as I took him into my mouth. He rolled me over and I spread my legs to welcome him inside me. We began slowly and then picked up speed, wonderful speedy thrusts. A seagull on our windowsill happily screeched his approval as we came to a positively explosive mutual orgasm, our *Mountaintop*. Bob gave the bird a name—*Climax*.

As we got out of the shower after an hour of incredible sex, the phone rang. It was Ralph Norquist. I invited him and Marlene to join us for dinner at *The Palm East Hampton*. I hoped he didn't notice that I was out of breath.

We've always enjoyed staying at the Norquists' house in East Hampton, but the place we recently bought was, well, huge. We took them on a tour of the entire house. Ralph and Marlene freaked out over it, especially the views.

"Our place is like a little cabin compared to this. I think I'll write a book," Ralph said. "What did you tell me your advance was? $15 million if I recall."

"Go for it, Ralph. Bob and I will happily serve as your first-round editors. With your name, you'll have a ready-made market."

We walked into the *Palm East Hampton* shortly after six. Because it was early and not quite at the height of the season, the place wasn't crowded.

We were shown to a table in the back, as I had requested.

Anytime we meet with Ralph, the subject always gets around to business, so I figured a little privacy was a good idea, and the table in the back worked. Rather than avoid talking business, Bob and I brought them up to date on what had been happening at the CIA. We knew we could speak openly around Marlene. She's discreet and she gets it. Also, the campus riots were anything but secret, so we spoke freely.

Marlene is a professor of English at the City College of New York. She's a tall, pretty woman with light green eyes and graying brunette hair. She's also beautifully slim, which I found surprising from the way she chowed down.

"So, how's everything at City College, Marlene?" I asked, afraid of what I was about to hear.

"I haven't been to class in three weeks, because there haven't *been* any classes. Ralph tells me you're his best detectives. I hope you guys can do something about this crap. I've been teaching college for 30 years, and I never could have imagined what's going on. These creeps aren't protesting anything—they just want to shut us down. Kids are dropping out in droves and getting menial jobs rather than sit around in the student union building playing board games or reading novels. Student loan applications are way down, because nobody wants to risk being saddled with gigantic debt, not knowing if they'll get a degree to justify it. Ralph tells me this crap is orchestrated, like a war of some sort. Do you folks agree with Ralph? Don't worry, you can disagree with the boss if you're so inclined."

I laughed at Marlene's comment about disagreeing with the boss. Bob and I always feel free to disagree with Ralph, one of the reasons we enjoy working for him. But we didn't disagree at all, especially after what we've found out recently.

"No, Marlene," I said, "We don't disagree with Ralph one bit. This lunacy we're seeing is orchestrated, carefully orchestrated. And the goal is to shut the country down by first shutting down higher education."

"I haven't seen you two in a few days," Ralph said. "Are you at liberty to disclose what you've learned or is there a 'need to know' issue? Knowing you two, I'm sure you've learned a lot."

"Actually, Ralph, and this may surprise you, the CIA's position is to make as much of this as public as possible. Director Buster wants the country to know what's going on and who's causing it. That's President Fenton's position as well."

"So, don't keep us in the dark, Bobbie," Marlene said. "Who the hell are these people?"

"Does the name Randolfo Martin ring a bell?"

"Holy shit," Ralph announced loudly, turning a few heads in the restaurant. "None other than the son of the former President of the United States, that evil bastard Bartholomew Martin, America's first and only dictator. I thought we were done with the delightful Martin family when Bartholomew was assassinated in prison and his other son, Antonio, was sentenced to life. Where is the son of a bitch Randolfo working from? Let me guess—Iran?"

Bob and I cracked up. Ralph has a way of nailing conclusions accurately.

"Yes, Iran," I said, "Tehran specifically. Randolfo knows how to pick bodyguards."

"How did you find out it's him?" Ralph asked. "From what the CIA and FBI tell me, he's the most secretive bastard on the planet."

"We got it from a prisoner whom Bob and I interrogated at the CIA."

"Why does that not surprise me?" Ralph said, laughing. "When the BBs interrogate somebody, information flows like a river. Is it some sort of organization?"

"A few of our interrogees characterized it as a 'movement.' It's called EOA or *End of America*. The very name of the organization tells us what their aim is. Yes, it's accurate to say that we're at war."

"And my students and I are on the field of battle," Marlene said.

CHAPTER FORTY-NINE

The *MV World Odyssey* cast off its lines from the Broadway Pier in San Diego. Built in Germany in 1998, the ship was originally named the *Deutschland*. The ship now serves as the seagoing "campus" of the "Semester at Sea," an educational program run by Colorado State University. It isn't a huge vessel by cruise ship standards. She's 575 feet in length, with a 76-foot beam, and can accommodate 600 students. The ship has 10 decks and nine classrooms. Anyone who wants to attend classes on the Semester at Sea had better reserve early, because the classes were always completely booked.

This voyage would last 106 days, and the ship would visit 11 countries, 12 cities, and 4 continents.

Sergeant Jerome Patterson commanded a platoon of six U.S. Army soldiers, stationed on the ship on orders from the new Director of Campus Security, General Mike Bennett. One of Bennett's main administrative tasks was to assign military units to college and university campuses, including floating ones. According to a Gallup poll, the vast majority of the American people thought that President Fenton made a great move by appointing General Mike as Director of Campus Security.

The first classes were scheduled for Monday morning.

Nineteen-year-old Melanie Tompkins, a sophomore at Cornell University, sipped coffee with her friend and fellow Cornell student, Clair Bixby.

"I cannot friggin believe this, Claire. I feel like I'm in heaven. My parents are the two greatest people in my life, and they gave me this Semester at Sea as a reward for making dean's list last semester. I love sea travel."

"Did their decision have anything to do with all the goddam campus riots, Melanie? I know it had a lot to do with my folks signing me up for this cruise."

"Yeah, they're both so fed up with all the violent bullshit, I think they would have yanked me out of school if this Semester at Sea wasn't an option. Cornell has seen its share of riots recently. I doubt we'll see any of those so-called 'demonstrations' out here on the ocean. My God, just think, Mel, we'll actually attend classes. How refreshing."

"Hey, to change the subject, Claire, have you noticed that a lot of our fellow students speak with heavy Arab accents? One guy I tried to start a conversation with didn't speak a word of English, not one goddam word."

"Maybe he was just trying an imaginative way to flirt with you."

"Wise guy. The little shrimp barely came up to my shoulders. Hey, what's that noise?"

They heard a chant coming from the deck below. *Colorado State, a place of hate, Colorado State, a place of hate, Colorado State, a place of hate...*

"Holy shit, Claire, do you think we're hearing a fucking demonstration? Class starts in 20 minutes. Do you think it will happen?"

"Mel, this sounds awfully familiar. Let's go to class. It's below on deck three in classroom 301. Let's see if we can find seats."

They took the escalator down to deck three. They passed room 303, another classroom. The hallway outside of room 303 was occupied by about 25 people with placards, all chanting "Colorado State, a place of hate." They continued down the passageway to classroom 301 where their English literature class was about to begin. Another group of placard-waving chanters occupied the space outside the room. Claire and Melanie carefully made their way to the classroom, weaving in and out of the "demonstrators." They walked in and took their seats.

Professor Barbara Dimitri stood at the front of the room behind a lectern and addressed the class. Nobody could hear a word she said because of the throaty chanting in the hallway. *Colorado State, a place of hate,* etc. etc. Professor Dimitri is a short woman at 5'3." Her pretty face left no doubt that she was furious. She walked to the door and stepped into the hallway. "Hey, do you mind?" she screamed, "I'm trying to teach a class."

Melanie couldn't believe what she saw next. The little professor almost flew backwards into the classroom, landed flat on her back, her nose bleeding badly, obviously from having been punched. Instinctively, Melanie ran to the door, slammed it shut and locked it. The screaming and chanting continued unabated, now accompanied by the sound of objects slamming against the bulkheads. Melanie had some medical background when she worked as an EMT at her father's ambulance company. She ran to Professor Dimitri, who was now sitting up, stanching the blood from her nose with a handkerchief. Her dress was covered in blood. Melanie stared at the woman's face and realized that her nose was broken. Dimitri had also cracked her head against the floor when she fell backwards. Melanie advised her to remain seated, for fear that she may have suffered a concussion as well as a broken nose.

Sergeant Patterson ran to deck three along with two other soldiers from his six-man platoon. They carried M16 assault rifles, armed with rubber bullets. His orders were to use force to prevent violence, but to avoid lethal force if possible. He shouted, "Stand down, backs against the wall."

Melanie heard him and opened the door a crack. "In here please, soldier." His two corporals kept their guns trained on the crowd as he walked into the classroom. He introduced himself.

"Look at this, Sergeant," Melanie said. "Those bastards broke this poor woman's nose."

Although his orders were to avoid lethal force, he did have the option to do so if a civilian is injured or attacked. He decided it was time to exercise that option. He removed the rubber bullet magazine from his M16 and slammed in a new magazine of live ammunition.

"Everyone stay right here until further notice," he shouted to the students and the bloody Professor Dimitri. The chanting in the hallway had resumed. *Colorado State, a place of hate, Colorado State, a place of hate,* and so on.

As he walked into the hallway with his M16 at the ready, one of the demonstrators lunged at him with a bat. Patterson opened fire, and the man's lifeless body fell to the deck. He told the two soldiers to remain with their guns trained on the crowd. He also told them to replace their rubber bullet magazines with live ammunition. Patterson then went to the ship's bridge and sent out a radio signal with a code sign to three American warships that steamed nearby. Part of his job was to remain aware of any U.S. Navy ships in the vicinity and to call them in the event of violence.

Within 20 minutes, the American destroyer, *USS Vincennes* approached the *World Odyssey*. A helicopter launched from the *Vincennes* and landed on the afterdeck of the ship. Six heavily armed Marines jumped to the deck, reinforcements for Sergeant Patterson's beleaguered soldiers. Assisted by the Marines, the ship's master at arms placed all the demonstrators under custody because some of them had engaged in violence, clear grounds for arrest. They would be held at the movie theater in the aft end of the ship, guarded by the heavily armed Marines. Part of the curriculum of the Semester at Sea program called for movies in the ship's theater every night. It wouldn't happen as scheduled, because the theater was now a makeshift jail.

The Semester at Sea program would conduct no classes that day.

CHAPTER FIFTY

Judge Sheila McCrary was the Chief Bankruptcy Judge for the Southern District of New York. John Roberts, Chief Justice of the United States Supreme Court, had appointed Judge McCrary to take on a new role in addition to her regular judicial duties. It was now her job to monitor and oversee bankruptcy filings by any American colleges or universities. She was in a meeting with David Abrams, her chief law clerk.

"David, I'm concerned. To be more accurate, I'm scared shitless." Judge McCrary is known for her salty tongue. "I just reviewed the total bankruptcy filings of colleges and universities this morning. Dear Lord, no fewer than 1,275 institutions have filed for bankruptcy. We know what that means for some small towns and cities where those colleges are located. It will have the same effect as if a major manufacturing plant closed. Lights out. These fucking demonstrations are taking a toll, a heavy toll."

"I don't think of them as demonstrations, your honor, I think of them as riots. My sister is a sophomore at Yale. She hasn't attended class in a month—because there were no classes to attend. As we read from the filing papers, the financial picture is bleak. Parents across the country are pulling their kids out of school, because they see no purpose in attending. Judge, I think it's obvious that somebody is trying to shut down our entire system of higher education. My God,

I just heard about that Semester at Sea program run by Colorado State. There was a riot on their ship just last week. A riot on a ship, of all places."

"All we can do is monitor this shit, David, which is my job. This is the most depressing judicial assignment I've ever had. And it doesn't look like the picture is going to improve anytime soon. Just yesterday there were 25 more demonstrations, or as you put it more accurately, riots. You and I have our degrees, David, but a lot of these poor kids will never see a college diploma. People are beginning to see college enrollment as the equivalent of shooting craps. I just hope to hell the government is getting a handle on this situation."

CHAPTER FIFTY-ONE

G ood evening, ladies and gentlemen, I'm Leslie Stahl for *60 Minutes*. Tonight, we're going to take another look at the shocking and compelling drama that is unfolding at our nation's college and university campuses. Last week my colleague, Bill Whitaker, interviewed five college presidents about the situations on their campuses, and we were shocked to hear their stories, tales of class cancellations and wanton violence. People who tuned to *60 Minutes* were treated to a horror story.'

"In this edition of *60 Minutes*, we're going to look at how law enforcement is handling the problem. The right to protest is so fundamental to our way of life that it almost doesn't bear repeating. But what we've been seeing over the past few months goes beyond simple protest demonstrations. In far too many instances, the protests have turned to violence, horrible violence. And nobody has come forward to explain what the *protests* were about. Demonstrations are turning into full-blown riots.

"So how do we balance our sacred right to protest with our equally important right to personal safety? That is the subject of this evening's segment of *60 Minutes*. Joining us this evening are two well-known police detectives, Bobbie Nelson and her husband and detective partner, Bob Lawton. In an article in *The New York Times* entitled, 'The BBs – New York City's Dynamic Detective Duo,' their famous nickname, *the BBs*, made its public debut. Bobbie and Bob were partnered as detectives less than two years ago. Within a couple of months after they began their partnership, they married, becoming partners in more ways than one.

"Having spent some time with them before the show, I can tell you they are probably the closest couple I've ever met. They finish each other's sentences and even communicate with just a glance or a gesture. I think it's accurate to describe them as a couple of law enforcement lovebirds. They're famous for solving difficult cases, both before and after they were partnered. It was no surprise that NYPD Commissioner Ralph Norquist assigned them one of the toughest cases imaginable, the campus riots. To handle this assignment, Bobbie and Bob have also been sworn in as provisional CIA and FBI agents, giving them jurisdiction in other states.

"Welcome to *60 Minutes*, Bob and Bobbie. Please give us your opinions on these campus demonstrations, which some people have simply branded as riots. Bobbie?"

"Law enforcement is involved in these matters for two reasons," Bobbie said. "First is because of the violence, which has begun to spin out of control. The other reason cops are involved is that we suspect that these incidents are not spontaneous protests but are meticulously coordinated criminal activities."

"And who is at the top of this pyramid?" Leslie asked. "Is one person or group organizing these activities?"

"It's a group, often referred to as a *movement*, and yes, one person is at the top," Bob said.

"Are you at liberty to tell us who this person is?"

"We have conclusive evidence that the man heading this up is none other than Randolfo Martin, the son of the infamous Bartholomew Martin, the former President of the United States, the

149

infamous dictator. His brother Antonio, you may recall, is serving a life sentence in prison. The group even has a shocking name—*End of America*."

"I must say I'm surprised that you were able to disclose his name to us."

"That came filtered to us right from the White House," Bob said. "President Fenton made it known to our superiors that he wants that information out in the open. He wants our country to know who we're up against, a ruthless tyrant. Unfortunately, he's hiding in a place over which we have no jurisdiction."

"A colleague of mine teaches a course at the Columbia School of Journalism," Leslie Stahl said, "or I should say *taught* a course, past tense. Classes haven't been held for six weeks because of the disturbances. I understand that's the case across the country. That group has taken it upon itself to force class cancellations. Can you tell what your investigations have disclosed about the *End of America*, which I understand is also referred to by its acronym, EOA?"

"We've discovered a lot, Leslie, from documentary evidence as well as countless interrogations, conducted by Bob and me as well as detectives and federal agents across the country. Simply put, *End of America*, and its leader Randolfo Martin, wants to put an end to our system of higher education, a key part of our culture as well as a major component of our economy. I believe President Fenton was accurate when he said that a war has been declared on the United States."

"And President Fenton has taken the shocking step of suspending the Posse Comitatus Act, thereby allowing our armed forces to act in civilian settings," Stahl said. "Any thoughts on that, Bob?"

"It may have been a radical step, but I don't think he had much choice," Bob said. "The NYPD, along with police departments across the country, simply doesn't have enough officers to respond to riots and at the same time carry on normal police functions. This campus violence has turned the country on its head."

"That ends our show for tonight, Ladies and gentlemen. I think I speak for us all when I say that I feel safer knowing that the BBs, Bobbie Nelson and Bob Lawton are *on the case.*

"Tune in next week for another edition of *60 Minutes.*"

CHAPTER FIFTY-TWO

Bob

I think our appearance on *60 Minutes* may help move the case forward. I was surprised when President Fenton let it be known that he wanted us to disclose the name of Randolfo Martin. At least it lets the country know who we're up against, a ruthless tyrant, or an "evil scumbag" as the First Lady puts it. I think Fenton was wise to take off the security wraps. The more people who are aware of this man, the better.

Bobbie and I enjoyed our brief stay at our beautiful home in East Hampton. We both agreed that having a place to get away, even if only for a couple of days, was a wonderful way to relieve stress. And we sure had a wonderful time relieving it, with almost nonstop love making. We're in a war against a brutal enemy, but we agreed that we shouldn't let the bastards control our lives. Bobbie and I have decided that we're going to live our lives, despite the shit we have to deal with.

Detectiving, our best-selling book, has been taking off like a rocket. It's been number one on *The New York Times* Nonfiction Best Seller list for 11 weeks. Our advance of $15 million has long since been paid back, and now we were enjoying royalties of almost $100,000 a month. The sales have also helped bring my novel *Army of Blue* back into the sunlight, and it's raking in royalties of $25,000 a month. Our book royalty bucks happily coincided with an email message I received this morning. I'm dying to tell Bobbie about it.

Bobbie just walked in, having gone to the records office to retrieve a file.

"Hey, Bobbie, you and I have been complaining about the size of our apartment lately. Any more thoughts on that?"

"Yeah, I'm conflicted as hell, honey. I love that we're so close to the office, and the place really is pretty, but when we return from East Hampton, I feel like we're living in a shoebox."

"Well, baby, I got a wonderful email this morning. Our next-door tenant, Tom Ralston, informed me that he and his wife won't be renewing their lease when it expires next month. They have an option to extend it for a year, but they're waiving that option."

"Oh, my God!"

"Yeah, oh my God. If we break down the wall, we'll have a huge 3,000 square foot apartment. We can put in a hot tub and a pool table—yes, a pool table. I don't need to tell you what *that* means. With the extra rooftop space, we'll be able to construct a running track, a rooftop garden, and an outdoor dining area just like that beautiful place we stayed in when we were in the Witness Protection Program."

"This is a fabulous idea, honey! Thank God for our book royalties."

"Speaking of book royalties, you and I need to get cooking on our next project."

"What's that?"

"Let's do some additions and renovations to our house in East Hampton. Hell, the way our book royalties are rolling in, we can easily afford renovations as well as redesign our city apartment.

Let's do it."

She walked over to me and stroked my face. Then she picked up the phone.

"Who are you calling.?"

"Tim Brady, that architect guy we've become friends with. We need to meet with him so he can start drawing up plans. I just read in the *Times* that he got an award from *Architectural Digest* for apartment designs."

When Bobbie gets on a roll, she likes to keep rolling.

"Bob and Bobbie," our assistant said before Bobbie could dial, "click on the TV." Bobbie put down the phone.

"George Stephanopoulos for *ABC News*, ladies and gentlemen. Our national crisis of campus violence continues unabated. Last week President Fenton, in a controversial move, suspended the Posse Comitatus Act of 1878, which was intended to keep American armed forces from intervening in civilian matters. But, in my opinion, he really had no choice. Our nation's police forces simply don't have the manpower to deal with the constant riots. And, as we reported yesterday, no place seems safe from armed protesters.

"The cruise ship *World Odyssey* serves as the ocean-going campus for the Colorado State University program, Semester at Sea. True to form, what is referred to as a 'demonstration' broke out on the ship just before the first planned morning classes. The demonstration soon turned violent as one of the protesters punched a woman professor in the face, breaking her nose.

"The embarked Army platoon responded to the scene, and the sergeant in command shot and killed a man who charged him with a bat. Marine reinforcements from a nearby destroyer stormed aboard, and the protesters are now being held under armed guard in the ship's theater.

"The soldiers were aboard on orders from retired Marine General Michael Bennett, whom President Fenton recently appointed to a new position known as Director of Campus Security. The office is part of the Department of Homeland Security. General Bennett briefly served as president of New York University, until his appointment by President Fenton as Director of Campus Security. *The World Odyssey* is headed for its homeport in San Diego, California, where its cargo of violent demonstrators will be taken into FBI custody.

"We have received reports that the organization behind these violent demonstrations is known as *End of America*, or its acronym, EOA. And, as we learned recently, the man who heads up that EOA program is none other than Randolfo Martin, the son of the former President of the United States, and America's only dictator, Bartholomew Martin. President Fenton, wisely in my opinion, has chosen to make the information public.

"Ladies and gentlemen, as President Fenton said when he declared the national state of emergency, 'America is at war,' a war not of our choosing, but a war that is being brutally waged by some strange force. *ABC* will keep you up to date on these bizarre developments.

"In other news…"

"So, what do you think, baby?" I said.

"I think I'm going to do what I was about to do before that TV announcement. I'm going to call our architect friend to start plans for our apartment. Bob, you and I know how to handle tough cases and we'll handle this one. But I'll be dipped in shit before I put our lives on hold because of Randolfo Martin's creeps."

"You're even more beautiful when you're angry."

"Well, I'm so angry maybe I should run for Miss America."

CHAPTER FIFTY-THREE

Bobbie

Wartime Bobbie Nelson here. Yeah, wartime, all because of an evil bastard named Randolfo Martin. I've only fired my weapon once in the line of duty, when I shot the man who tried to assassinate Bob. But I would love to empty an entire magazine into the skull of that slimy animal, Randolfo Martin. He's trying to destroy the American higher education system, and along with it the country itself. He seems well on his way. But he's going to have to come through the BBs to do it. Maybe Bob and I should start our own movement, EOR, or *End of Randolfo*. Fuck him.

But, as I often remind Bob—and myself—anger is an emotion that gets you nowhere, even though Bob tells me I look pretty when I'm angry. But anger does help to focus you on your mission, and our mission is to stop that ruthless bastard. I think President Fenton got it right to declare a national emergency and appoint General Mike as Director of Campus Security. I really like General Mike, and, God knows, he's a big fan of Bob. So am I.

Bob looks especially cute this morning, but I always think he does. His lightly starched white shirt highlighted his gorgeous physique. Maybe we can play a game of strip billiards later. Oh, right, we don't have a pool table—yet. Maybe strip poker? Hey, time to get to work.

"Bob and Bobbie," our assistant said, "CIA Director Buster is here."

Buster never tires of surprising people.

Buster walked in and gave each of us a bear hug. We're becoming really good friends with this guy. He looked like he hadn't slept in a week, and I told him he's been working too hard. Maybe he should buy a house in East Hampton, but he probably can't afford it. Hey, write a book! Okay, time to pay attention.

The three of us walked over to the small conference table.

"Coffee? You have a choice of decaf or regular."

"Decaf, please. My nerves are jangled enough. To get right to the point, I need you guys at CIA for a couple of days. How about starting tomorrow?"

I remembered that Bob and I are scheduled to meet with the architect tomorrow to start working on plans for our new apartment—the one that will have a hot tub—and a pool table.

"How about the day after tomorrow, Buster?"

"Fine. We have a new group of guests we've captured—don't ask me how we capture people, okay? There are eight of them and I want you guys to pump them for information. You two amaze me the way you climb inside an interrogee's head. We have some great spooks at the CIA, but nobody can hold a candle to the BBs when it comes to interrogation."

He was being really sweet and flattering, but he's also correct—*nobody* interrogates people like Bob and me.

"Are we looking for anything specific," Bob asked, "or just to see whatever information we can get?"

"Good question, Bob. We have what we think is the most important intelligence. We know that the top dog is Randolfo Martin."

"You mean the top *scumbag*," I interrupted, embarrassing myself.

Buster just laughed. He knows me by now.

"We also know that he's in Tehran, and we know what EOA means," Buster said. "We also have a pretty good handle on how these demonstrations play out—and that they're becoming increasingly violent. So, here's my point. Suppose, just suppose, we removed the man at the top…"

"You mean whack the son of a bitch?" I inquired.

"Well, something like that," Buster said with a wink. "What we really want to know is how deep the philosophy, if you can call it that, goes. In other words, is this just a Randolfo Martin show, or will the participants carry on without him? If we find it's a Randolfo command performance, that makes things easier, because the rioters will eventually disperse without his leadership. Randolfo Martin appears to be calling the shots, but we need to know if there's anyone else on the management team."

"But that would be speculation," Bob said.

"Well, it bothers me too, Bob," Buster said, "but not much. Hell, President Fenton has taken the gloves off, and General Mike, his newly appointed Director of Campus Security, knows how to kick ass. And you two have seen me in action. You know that I play rough—*very rough*. If these 'demonstrators' try to carry on without their charismatic leader, we'll have them on the run in no time."

"Bob and I have discussed this a lot, Buster. Do you see much sympathy for these creeps, even though they don't seem to protest anything specific at all?"

"Besides us and the rest of the government, do you know who else is really pissed off? The American people. I just read a *Fox*

News poll, which clearly indicated they've had it up to their ears with this shit. I think a lot of people will be ready to hold our jackets for this fight. The last thing I'd ever want to see is martial law, but that's where these bastards are pointing us. Okay, I gotta run. See you folks in Langley the day after tomorrow."

After Buster left, we sat there with our thoughts.

"You know what we should do, honey?" I said.

"We should have a nice dinner and then go to a musical comedy."

"Perfect idea. I love you, Bob."

CHAPTER FIFTY-FOUR

Bob

Bobbie and I walked to our apartment where we'd have lunch with Tim Brady, our architect friend. We didn't want to meet in a restaurant because, knowing Tim as we do, he would already have some preliminary drawings for us and would want to spread them out on the dining room table. Bobbie had already given him the bare bones of our idea—knock down a wall and double the size of our apartment. We've had Tim and his wife over to our place a few times before, so he knew the layout in his head. Bobbie ordered a delicious lunch from a gourmet deli around the corner. She may not know how to cook, but she sure knows how to place an order.

When I opened the door to let Tim in, he looked like he just won the lottery.

"Oh, my God, this is going to be fun!" he yelled.

"Does that mean you're not going to charge us?" Bobbie said, laughing.

"Of course, it doesn't mean that. Hey, fun and money go together."

He spread his drawing out on the dining room table.

"I have a good memory for physical spaces," Tim said, "so these plans are based in my recollections, without precise measurements, of course."

Bobbie and I were shocked at what he had come up with in just two days, without measuring anything. Bobbie had told him that the apartment next door was almost a cookie cutter image of our place, except with an opposite layout. He didn't so much redesign the apartment—he reinvented it. He removed one kitchen and doubled the size of the other one. He expanded the master bath and included a huge hot tub. Next to the den, he set aside space for a pool table. We had made it clear to him that we wanted space for a pool table. We didn't mention our plans to play *Strip Billiards*. He even designed a small theater on a sloping platform to mimic the experience of a real playhouse. He also put in a modest sized gym. Although he had no measurements at all, he did a rough sketch of our rooftop running track, garden, and outside dining area.

So, fuck Randolfo Martin, as Bobbie loves to say. The BBs are getting on with our lives. We'll worry about Tehran later.

But we'd soon find out that Tehran requires us to worry—*now*.

CHAPTER FIFTY-FIVE

Deputy Foreign Minister Hamid Rashadi met with his colleague, Minister Ramin Abbasi, at his office in Tehran. The two had been close friends for years, ever since they served together in the Iranian Army. They are both high level officials in the Iranian government. Many, especially those best described as "moderates," hope to see Rashadi as the next prime minister after Ali Khamenei. The subject of their meeting was the new "guest" of the Iranian government, Randolfo Martin.

Rashadi's office was large at 25 by 30 feet. All of the furniture was plush leather, Rashadi's favorite type of decorating. The sun streamed in from the window overlooking a courtyard, casting the room in a pleasant glow. The walls were decorated with paintings of pastoral scenes by Hudson River School artists, his favorite school of art. Rashadi reached under his desk and grabbed a bottle of Kentucky bourbon. He poured them both a healthy splash.

"Ramin, we have known each other a long time, and we both know that Iran has a sudden problem on its hands, a huge problem. Prime Minister Khamenei insists on spouting his crazy slogan about America as *The Great Satan*. Although we'd never discuss it with anyone other than ourselves, Ramin, we both know that *The Great Satan* should really be seen as our *Great Friend*. Our "guest," as Khamenei refers to Randolfo Martin, is every bit as insane as his late father, Bartholomew. And he's using that group *End of America* as a tool to destroy the American educational system. And we're harboring the son of a bitch. What say you, my friend?"

"Hamid, I share your concern about this matter. As you know, I have met President Fenton and his brilliant wife, Meg. President Fenton is a steady leader and a thoughtful man, but not one to be trifled with. When he served in the American Navy, he was known as a fighting admiral, never one to shy away from combat. And Randolfo Martin is doing the last thing you would ever want to risk with a brave man like Fenton. He's pushing him into a corner, giving him no other option than to come out fighting. And our prime minister is coddling Randolfo Martin, that evil bastard. Khamenei sees anyone who opposes America as our ally. As we both know, nothing could be further from the truth. What will happen if the United States declares war on Iran?"

Rashadi poured them both another healthy splash of bourbon.

"We both know the answer to that question, Hamid. It will mean the destruction of our country. And all because our supreme leader allows Randolfo Martin to do as he pleases. If President Fenton chooses the military option, I expect to see the overwhelming majority of the American people supporting his actions. The Americans are outraged at seeing colleges and universities turned into scenes of riots. They spend their hard-earned money on tuition, and their sons and daughters don't even have the opportunity to attend class. Have you been in touch with our friend…?"

"Please, Ramin, don't mention his name, even in this room. But, to answer your question, yes, I have been in touch with him."

"That's good. Buster will figure out a solution to this problem, my friend."

CHAPTER FIFTY-SIX

Bobbie

I mildly freaked out over Tim Brady's plans for our expanded apartment. Well no, not mildly freaked out—totally freaked out. That guy really knows his stuff. Wait till he takes measurements! So, the place may not be like our house in East Hampton, but 3,000 square feet plus a rooftop track, garden, and outdoor dining area is not bad. And we'll still be right near One PP. God bless book royalties.

Buster sent a CIA Gulfstream to pick up Bob and me for our trip to Langley. Wow, do these government types know how to spend taxpayer money. A Gulfstream? Why not economy seats on a regular flight? Bob and I agreed that we felt like we were in an episode of *Criminal Minds,* where a group of FBI agents shuttle around in a Gulfstream. We landed at the old Langley Air Force Base, now charmingly known as Joint Base Langley-Eustis, a short drive from CIA headquarters.

Our assignment was to interrogate eight people who were "invited" by the CIA. We figured it would take the better part of two days to do our questioning. We were happy to see our old friend Marcia Barrett, CIA agent, Arabic/Farsi interpreter, and ass-kicker-on-call.

We met Marcia for breakfast at one of the agency cafeterias, where the food was quite good, as Bob and I had learned from our previous visits. All three of us had breakfasts low on carbs, as it's important to be alert when interrogating prisoners. We decided that we would get right into our interrogees' heads, as Buster would say. We would ask questions, all of which were a variation of—"What are you demonstrating against and who do you take orders from?"

Our first guest was Muhammed Alkaldi, who had been arrested at the University of Illinois-Urbana for throwing a punch at a cop during a "demonstration." He was advised, as were all the others, that his cooperation would result in leniency. How Buster would provide leniency I didn't know, nor did I care.

"Mr. Alkaldi, I understand that you were arrested on June 2nd at the University of Illinois during what is best described as a demonstration; is that correct?" He spoke perfect English, leaving Marcia to observe, which is fine by me. She's a damn good observer.

"Yes, but the police officer tried to punch me, I was only protecting myself."

I didn't doubt he was telling the truth, but it was irrelevant to our interrogation.

"Mr. Alkaldi, what were you demonstrating against?"

"Injustice."

"Can you be a bit more specific, sir?"

"The criminal American university system, as Sheik Randolfo advised us."

Sheik Randolfo? They even gave that low-life a title? I didn't show any emotion, Of course, although I sure as hell felt fear, and just continued my questioning.

"And can you tell us to what specific injustices this Sheik Randolfo fellow was referring?"

"Injustice against students."

"Such as?"

"Forcing them to attend class."

Don't argue, I reminded myself, even when hit by something that is patently absurd and made no sense whatsoever.

"Mr. Alkaldi, do you think that class attendance may be necessary for the students' education?" Sometimes I like to ask obvious questions.

"It is not necessary to advance the propaganda of the infidel."

I had a sudden desire to review our architect's plans for our new apartment, but I realized it was necessary to continue with this dipshit. I figured it was time to drive to the heart of the issue.

"Mr. Alkaldi, suppose, just suppose for the sake of speculation, that Sheik Randolfo decided to abandon his leadership of your group. Would you continue on without him?"

"The sheik would never abandon us."

"That was a hypothetical question, asshole," Marcia advised, "answer Detective Nelson's question." Marcia was fast becoming my favorite spook.

"So, to clarify my question, I am not saying Randolfo Martin *would* abandon you, but if he changed his mind what would you do?"

"I would await further orders."

"In other words, you wouldn't continue with your demonstrations until you got an order from Randolfo Martin, is that correct?"

"As I said, I would await further orders."

"But what if he gave you no further orders?"

"I would do nothing. Sheik Randolfo Martin is our leader."

"So, just to make sure I heard this correctly, without orders you would not demonstrate or participate in demonstrations?"

"That is correct. I would wait for orders."

"And just so I understand how this works; you receive specific orders from Sheik Randolfo, such as the one that got you arrested at the University of Illinois. Did he specifically order that demonstration?"

"He always gives us orders through one of the brothers who assists him,"

"Did he ever *personally* order a demonstration?"

"No, he does it through the brothers."

"Do you have a list of these brothers? In other words, how do you know the orders came from Randolfo Martin?"

"A brother would never lie to us."

Marcia slammed a file onto the desk.

"So, you don't even know who these brothers are, is that correct?"

"That is correct, I don't know their names."

"Mr. Alkaldi, did you ever hear the phrase 'blind obedience?'"

"Yes, blind obedience in the name of Allah."

"Thank you, Mr. Alkaldi. I don't have any further questions now, but we may need a follow-up meeting. An agent will return you to your cell."

Before our next interrogation, which Bob would conduct, I wanted to have a debriefing with Bob and Marcia.

"So, what do you guys think about this fucking robot?"

"Well, I have two observations," Bob said. "First, the guy insisted he doesn't demonstrate unless ordered to by Randolfo or someone on Randolfo's staff."

"Or who *says* he's from Randolfo's staff," Marcia said. *Good point.*

"Secondly," Bob said, 'this whole thing appears to be a Muslim show, a radical Muslim show, as we've suspected. But there's a problem with that. Randolfo Martin is not a Muslim, and he's said that publicly many times. He's using these people, and they don't seem to have a problem with that. I mean shit, the guy even referred to Randolfo as *Sheik*. Great job, Bobbie. I think we know where we're headed."

Bob thinks we know where we were headed. I wasn't so sure.

CHAPTER FIFTY-SEVEN

Bob

My job was to interrogate the next prisoner, Ali Multafi. Bobbie, as usual, did a great professional job questioning Mr. Alkaldi. The biggest piece of information she gathered is that the disciples will not continue with their demonstrations without the okay from Randolfo or one of his lieutenants. But those were the words of one man, one robot. If it's true that the lackeys only act on word from Tehran, that would certainly focus our options. And Buster is good selecting the right option.

The CIA agents who "invited" Mr. Multafi to come in for questioning believe that he's a leader in the ranks of the *End of America* people. They told Buster that they heard the man's name constantly in chatter.

"Good morning, Mr. Multafi. My name is Detective Bob Lawton, and I'm here to ask you a few questions."

"I have nothing to say to you."

"Listen to me, dickbrain," Marcia Barrett said with considerable volume in her voice, "unless you want to spend the rest of your wretched life in solitary confinement, I suggest that you answer Detective Lawton's questions."

I definitely want to recruit Marcia into the NYPD.

"Mr. Multafi, do you take orders from a man named Randolfo Martin?"

"Yes."

I questioned Multafi for two hours. His responses mimicked those of our first interrogee. Yes, Randolfo Martin is running the show, yes, they call him Sheik, and yes, he gives orders through his lieutenants.

And he's holed up safely in Tehran.

Bobbie, Marcia, and I continued our interrogation of the remaining six men. This interrogation wouldn't have moved so smoothly were it not for Marcia-the-ass-kicker. I got the impression that she scared the hell out of these guys. I agree with Bobbie that we should try to steal Marcia away from the CIA and recruit her into the NYPD. Our remaining interrogees told us pretty much the same as our first two: that the orders come from Randolfo, and the orders come through intermediaries, and the interrogee would not act without orders. But the last guy, Muhammed bin Hashim, had something to add, and he shocked the living shit out of us. He said that the *End of America* people would soon focus their demonstrations on high schools.

That could change everything.

CHAPTER FIFTY-EIGHT

President Harry Fenton sat in his private dining room at the White House, along with First Lady Meg. He loves to begin his day by having breakfast with Meg. He thinks of her as his one-woman cabinet. The subject of their meeting would be familiar, one that has begun their day for weeks—the *End of America* movement.

"Those two cops from New York who call themselves the BBs are simply unbelievable, Meg. Seeing them work is like watching a detective movie."

"I agree, honey. According to Sarah Watson, they're the best detectives she's ever seen, including her people at the FBI. And they sure as hell know how to dig up information. Have they given us anything new lately?"

"Yes, new. New and big. I just got word from Buster at the CIA that they've recently interrogated eight denizens of that weird EOA movement. I guess it should be no surprise, but that turd Randolfo Martin is not only pulling the strings, he completely controls all of the demonstrations that are tearing apart our country's campuses. And get this—one of the interrogees said that Martin is setting his sights on our high schools. You heard me, *high schools*."

"Oh my God, honey, this is getting out of control, if it hasn't already gotten out of control."

"And nothing happens unless the word comes from Randolfo Martin through one of his lieutenants."

"What do you think will happen next?"

"Take a deep breath, Meg. I wouldn't be surprised if Buster orders his people to have a 'talk' with Randolfo. You know what that means."

CHAPTER FIFTY-NINE

Bobbie

B ob and I were happy with our interrogations at the CIA over the past few days. Buster was beyond happy. We're all convinced that the *End of America* movement will not take any actions without explicit word from Randolfo Martin, issued through one of his henchmen. So, we know who holds the levers of power, but equally important, we know how the levers move. We began to feel confident that the *End of America* will soon end, largely because of the information we coaxed out of the prisoners.

We BBs know our stuff. So does our new CIA pal, Marcia Barrett.

We moved a few boxes of essentials from our apartment to a nearby Marriott Courtyard hotel. Construction on our new 3,000 square foot apartment will begin today, and we couldn't be happier. The Marriott is just a couple of blocks from our apartment, so we'll be able to visit regularly to check on the construction progress. Tim Brady's final plans for the apartment were perfect. We'll still be right near One PP, but we'll have some newfound luxury. Hey, if you can't enjoy money, why have it in the first place? Our room at the Marriott was fine by us, not luxurious, but neat, clean, and functional. And, it was still near One Police Plaza, just two blocks further than our apartment. It wasn't just a room but a small suite, with two bedrooms, two full baths, a den, and an eat-in kitchen. Our contractor estimates that the apartment will be finished in six weeks, so the Marriott will be our home for a while.

We met Ralph and Marlene Norquist at the diner for breakfast. They told us that they were going to their house in East Hampton for a few days, and suggested we take some time off to enjoy our new place. Wonderful suggestion, especially because it came from the boss.

Bob and I decided we would throw a party, our first get-together at our new waterfront home. But we wanted it to be a "working party." I think that sometimes we plan to work while we take a few days off, so we won't feel guilty about relaxing. Stupid, I know, but that's Bob and me. The BBs get antsy if we're not solving something.

We arrived at our house at 4:30 on Friday afternoon, looking forward to our party. We had recently hired a house cleaning service, and the place was spotless. The mid-September weather was perfect, in the high 60s, and the salty fragrance off Georgica Pond was bracing.

We invited Buster, who blew us away when he said he'd bring his wife, Peggy. We didn't even know Buster was married. He likes to keep his mouth shut about personal matters. He and Peggy arrived at 5:15. Peggy is a tall, strikingly pretty brunette. She's a CIA agent, not to our surprise. I couldn't help but notice that she had once suffered a broken nose, and it was still somewhat askew, although attractive in an odd way. Without prompting, she told us her nose was broken as she tried to arrest a suspect. She was unable to get medical attention for a couple of days, hence her slightly crooked nose. Peggy Atkins jokingly refers to herself as Peggy Buster. She and Buster will be staying over for the weekend. We also invited our new friend, CIA agent Marcia Barrett and her husband of three months, Bill Barrett, who is also a CIA agent. Marcia's first husband had been killed two years ago by a self-proclaimed jihadi. No wonder Marcia seems to harbor some angry shit about the gentlemen of the sand. Marcia and

Bill will be staying over as well. Commissioner Ralph and his wife Marlene would arrive shortly. Their house is a short walk from ours.

So, we all had a "need to know," which was good because we figured Buster would have some interesting things to tell us about *End of America*. Although she's not in law enforcement or espionage, we had no problem talking openly in front of Ralph's wife, Marlene. She's cool and discrete. We arranged for the dinner to be catered by the *Palm East Hampton*. We also hired a serving crew. I really should learn how to cook someday. Screw it—that's what telephones are for.

Bob served drinks from our sumptuous bar in the den.

Buster stood. "Folks, I wish to propose a toast to two of the most talented law enforcement people on the planet, the famous BBs. They're also fabulously talented authors, hence this lovely home, bought with book royalties."

Buster is so sweet, it's difficult to think of him as a hard-nosed spook. And he *is* hard-nosed, as we'd be reminded of shortly.

I was dying to get down to the status of our war, the war on our country, the *End of America*.

"Buster, why don't you tell us your thoughts about the interrogations that Bob, Marcia, and I conducted the other day," I suggested.

"Yeah," Bill Barrett joined in, "from what Marcia tells me it seems we have made some big headway on those *End of America* animals."

"Well, I'd like to hear Bob and Bobbie's thoughts on the subject," Buster said. "Their amazing interrogations, aided by Marcia here, have put us forward by light years. We now know that all marching orders for the demonstrations come straight from Randolfo Martin through his closest aides. Nothing happens unless it comes through Randolfo. He closely controls the strings, which didn't surprise me. So, Bob and Bobbie, your thoughts?"

"Bob and I think it's time your people had a 'talk' with Randolfo Martin, Buster. Your 'talks' always bring results."

Bob and I knew, and I'm sure the others did as well, that a Buster "talk" means somebody gets assassinated.

Bob walked to the bar and poured us another round of cocktails. He walked around the room serving the drinks from a tray. Bob is the perfect host. I think I'll send him to cooking school as a birthday present.

Buster stood and smiled. He raised his glass. "I propose another toast," he said, "to the end of the *End of America*. Yes, my people had a *talk* with Randolfo —five days ago."

Holy shit! Did Buster just tell us that he whacked that evil bastard?

The room went quiet. Did I hear correctly? Could it be that we now live in a Randolfo-free world?

"Is the war over, Buster?" Bob asked, his eyes like saucers.

"We'll know more as time goes by, but there hasn't been a campus demonstration in ten days. Not just a lack of riots, but no demonstrations at all. There's nobody at the top to pull the trigger."

The next morning, I was afraid to turn on the TV. But I also looked forward to it. My God, Randolfo Martin now resides underground, six feet underground.

CHAPTER SIXTY

Wolf Blitzer for *CNN* ladies and gentlemen. My job as a reporter is to do just that, to report the news. But sometimes the lack of news is a story in itself. Well, hang onto your hats, folks, because I'm pleased to say, for the first time in months, that there are no campus demonstrations to report. There hasn't been a violent demonstration in ten days. Actually, there haven't been any college or university demonstrations of any kind in ten days, violent or not. It's as if the people involved have decided to stop their criminal activities. For weeks we've been speculating whether the riots were planned from a central authority of some sort. If that's so, management of the *End of America* movement seems to have retired or taken a vacation. I give you this report with no small amount of trepidation on my part, because I hope I won't again start to report campus riots. But let's take good news when we can get it.'

"In other news…"

CHAPTER SIXTY-ONE

Bob

It's been two months since Buster told us about his operatives having a "talk" with Randolfo Martin. His inside moles have confirmed that Randolfo Martin is where he should be—in a grave. As NYPD detectives, Bobbie and I play by the rules. That said, we were delighted that Buster played by *his* rules. It's also been two months without a single incident of a demonstration or riot on any campus. Bobbie and I have returned to what we love, being cops, being detectives, finding patterns and solving puzzles. We were proud of our work as CIA spies, but now we return to the profession we're cut out for. We were back to *Detectiving*.

And we're delighted with our new 3,000 square foot apartment, into which we moved last month. Tim Brady's plans were exciting, but nothing like the finished product. It certainly isn't as big as our house in East Hampton, but 3,000 square feet is a huge apartment.

We just walked into Commissioner Ralph's office. He was smiling. He told us that he was delighted that his son had resumed attending classes at the University of Michigan.

He then handed us a file, a big file, another case. No surprise that it involved a serial killer. Fifteen bodies so far, and not one lead. This killer uses a gun. Or guns, I should say. He's careful to use a different gun for each killing in order to throw off our forensics. But we know it's a serial killer, because he always leaves a note on his victims—in ancient Greek. Looks like Bobbie will need to learn yet another language. The murders occur all over New York City, and, we were shocked to learn—at all times of the day.

I think Ralph likes to assign Bobbie and me tough cases. We love it when he does. The harder the puzzle, the more fun it is to solve, the more it requires the BBs style of *Detectiving*.

And Bobbie and I will handle this matter like we manage all of our cases—*together*.

RUSSELL F. MORAN

Characters – *The Streets of Terror*

Andrews, Marilyn – President of the Senior Council

Atkins, Peggy – Buster's wife

Barrett, Marcia – CIA Agent interrogator

Basak, Aarav – Internet scam artist

Bateman, Jenny – CEO, Robot Depot

Bennett, Mike – Retired Marine Corps General

Billings, Frank – Major, US Army Corps of Engineers

Browner, Henry (Hank) – MTA investigator

Buster – Director of the CIA, aka, Charles Atkins

Cummings, Phil – CIA Agent

Durmand, Max - Army colonel and prison commandant

Fenton, Harry – President of the United States

Fenton, Meg – First Lady of the United States

Flynn, Tom – Subway passenger

Lawton, Bob - NYPD Detective

Martin, Randolfo – Terrorist leader

Mussin, Ali – Terrorist and handyman at MetLife Stadium

Nelson, Bobbie – NYPD Detective

Norquist, Ralph – NYPD Commissioner

Paxton, Arnold – Mayor of New York City

Randolph, Joyce – Junior detective and assistant to Bob and Bobbie

Randolph, Mike – Joyce's husband

Rashadi , Hamid - Deputy Foreign Minister of Iran

Watson, Sarah – FBI Director

THE BOOKS OF RUSS MORAN

I hope you enjoyed reading *The Streets of Terror as* much as I enjoyed writing it.

This book, as well as all my books are available on Amazon.com, and also as ebooks on the Kindle or a Kindle app on your smartphone or iPad.

Here are my other books you may be interested in.

THE TIME MAGNET NOVELS
The Gray Ship – Book One *of the Time Magnet Novels*
http://amzn.to/16GPumH

A number one Amazon best seller.

"This **provocative, intensely powerful** *novel is a must-read for sci-fi fans and Civil War aficionados, though mainstream fiction readers will find it* **heart-rending and inspiring** *as well. A rare read that's not only* **wildly entertaining, but also profoundly moving."** – Kirkus Reviews

The Thanksgiving Gang – Book Two *of the Time Magnet Novels*
The Sequel to *The Gray Ship*. A story of time travel.
http://amzn.to/1NzBs7N

"I had never read a book before written in an efficient, minimalistic prose. Instead of writing what most readers want to read, he gives voice to life-like characters, with their flaws and prejudices. They are not infallible superheroes. It's always nice to find a new voice in fiction and to enjoy creativity at its best." – C. Ludewig

"Breakneck pacing and virtually nonstop action" – Kirkus Reviews

A Time of Fear – **Book Three** *of the Time Magnet Novels*
http://amzn.to/1zdjaG9

In a month, five American cities will be devastated by suitcase nuclear bombs.

The time travelers take on their old name, The Thanksgiving Gang. They know what will happen because they travelled to the future. They know what the result will be. They've seen the devastation. They know the details. Five American cities are targeted by nuclear suitcase bombs. BUT they don't know where the bombs are – and don't know how to find them. The clock is ticking, and millions will soon lose their lives – unless they find the bombs.

"His story is fascinating, and adds even more depth to this already cavernously deep novel. Amazingly unique, chilling and well written, Moran weaves a future that is both desperate and hopeful. Blending modern fears with science fiction results in a tale that will keep you reading long into the night. Five stars!" — Heather

The Skies of Time – **Book Four** *of the Time Magnet Novels*
http://amzn.to/1CCC3jg

In *The Skies of Time*, you will recognize the two main characters, Ashley Patterson, now an admiral, and her husband, Jack Thurber. They met and fell in love in *The Gray Ship*, and now they're in for the adventure of their lives in *The Skies of Time*. Ashley and Jack have been such prominent characters in all four books of The Time Magnet Series that I feel like they're old friends. You will also recognize some of the other characters. But if I told you who they are, it would ruin the fun.

"I'm big fan of this series and this one may be the best. I hope there is another book to this series since it keeps getting better. There are a few questions I have about certain events that makes the next

one even more suspenseful. These are great books to binge read one after the other." — Time Travel Fan

The Keepers of Time – Book Five *of the Time Magnet Novels*
http://amzn.to/2wjVSTt

Admiral Ashley Patterson and her husband Jack have done it again. They've traveled through time, 200 years into the future — aboard a nuclear aircraft carrier, the *USS Ronald Reagan*, Ashley's flagship.

They discover a new world, a strange new world — a post-nuclear war world — one that is both a beacon of hope, and a cry of despair.

They meet a group of people who call themselves *The Keepers of Time,* an organization dedicated to preserving history and culture amid the horrors of a dystopian future.

The world around them has harkened back to a primitive and savage past, one that includes human sacrifice.

Ashley knows they must have to get back to the present to warn the government of the unspeakable horrors that await. But finding the way back to the present is their greatest challenge, an almost insurmountable one.

"The Keepers of Time is a really interesting take on current geopolitical events and where they are leading. From reading previous books in the series, the cast of characters is as familiar as the people next door and it was great to reconnect with them. Moran's legal background illuminates what happens when our legal structure disappears, and he has zeroed in on an essential thing about civilization -- records of the past. A great read!" – Robert Shearer

THE PATTERNS SERIES
The Shadows of Terror – **Book One**
http://amzn.to/1IDQzJS

"A stunning page turner. A novel that explodes off the front page of your newspaper."

Terrorism has a new face, a face that's obscured in the shadows. The radical forces of destruction have learned to make themselves invisible to the West, and preventing a terrorist attack has become almost impossible. A new war has begun, World War III.

Rick Bellamy, an FBI agent who specializes in counterterrorism, is engaged in his own war, a war with no end. Bellamy's wife, Ellen, a prominent architect, discovers that she's in the middle of the greatest terror plot to date. To defeat the enemy, Bellamy first has to uncover the clues, to shine a light on the shadows. He has to find patterns – before it's too late.

"Move over James Patterson and Mary Higgins Clark. There's a new guy in town. Russ Moran's new book – The Shadows of Terror." — Frank O.

The Scent of Revenge - **Book Two** in *The Patterns Series*
http://amzn.to/2tneIsg

The world is at war with the forces of terror. FBI Agent Rick Bellamy and his wife, Ellen, find themselves in the middle of a sinister terrorist plot. Someone is attacking prominent young women, inflicting a horrible disease. Nobody knows its origin, nobody knows how to stop it, nobody knows how to cure it.

Rick Bellamy and a team of scientists want to go on the offense. But how?

Will the lives of the women be changed forever? When will the attacks stop?

"Heart-pounding can't put down thriller that will force you to look at terrorism in different light. Life in America will never be the same." – Cold Coffee Café

A Reunion in Time – Book Three of *The Patterns Series*
http://amzn.to/2tneIsg

What if a 37-year-old adult travels back 20 years in time and finds himself in high school, followed by his 36-year-old wife? They're now teenagers, 17 and 16. Adults in teenage bodies, they struggle to convince the people from their past that they are real, not apparitions. With the benefit of hindsight, they know the history of the past 20 years, and it isn't pretty.

Rick and Ellen are married, and now must adjust to married life as teenagers in 2001. Rick is a senior FBI official and Ellen is a famous architect.

But everybody sees them as kids. Nobody believes that they're married, and nobody believes their stories—until Rick and Ellen predict 9/11.

How do they find their way back to the year they came from? How do they warn the authorities of the cataclysm that will occur in the future? The answer is to find the time portal—the wormhole—that brought them to 2001. But the site has changed. It's no longer the place where they crossed the wormhole. Will they live out the balance of their lives beginning as teenagers?

"We've all wished we could go back to earlier times with the mind we have now. This Moran book takes you there and it is a fun creative romp well worth reading. A Reunion in Time is highly recommended!" – Kindle customer

THE MATT BLAKE MYSTERIES
Sideswiped – **Book One of** *The Matt Blake Mysteries, a series of* **legal thrillers**
http://amzn.to/1MkxX35

Trial lawyer Matt Blake took on a perfect case. It involved a sideswipe collision in which his client's husband, an investigative reporter, was killed. The evidence of negligence was overwhelming. Eyewitnesses testified that defendant was talking on his cell phone when he hit the other car.

But was it negligence? Was it an accident? Or was it murder?

Matt uncovers evidence that the act may have been intentional. Somebody wanted the man silenced. Somebody wanted the man dead. Somebody had a lot to hide. The signs started to point to the highest levels of government. An open-and-shut personal injury case suddenly became a vast conspiracy of terror.

"This book hooks you in from the first line. Sideswiped draws you into the world of Matt Blake and you become emotionally attached to him and his journey. The story itself is so well-written and moves quickly. There is never a dull moment." – Sarah Elle

"Moran demonstrates the depth of his writing talent by developing a new genre with Sideswiped, a legal thriller. Branching out from his previous novels dealing with time travel, Moran goes in a whole new direction with Book One in the Matt Blake series. He creates a wild but totally believable story of modern-day intrigue and suspense. Moran also deftly weaves into this book some of my favorite characters from his prior novels. I am looking forward to starting Book #2 - The Reformers." – Frank from Lynbrook, NY

The Reformers – Book Two of *The Matt Blake Mysteries*
http://amzn.to/2m8uMdu

The forces of radical Islam are on the run. Their leadership has been decimated, their ranks thinned, their power disappearing by the week. Their recruiting efforts have been cut off, the radical websites shut down, and the attraction of jihad is losing its appeal among the young. With targeted assassinations, military strikes, as well as the loss of oil fields and gold mines, radical Islam is fast losing power.

But who is responsible? It isn't the United States Government. It's a new force the world has never seen before.

Lawyer Matt Blake and his wife Diana find themselves in the middle of the most gigantic plot the world has ever seen, a conspiracy that's only begun to grow.

"I've been a fan of the author, Russell Moran, since reading Sideswiped a few months ago, so I admittedly went into this book with quite high expectations. That being said, I had no idea that "The Reformers" was going to play out in the way that it does and I can see myself giving this book a re-read in the future. In fact, I am even more impressed by the storyline of this read than the last and it has left me excited to see more." – Lucidity.

"Time flies when you're scared out of your mind. The author's superb writing skills will quickly draw you into the story. Forty-two fast paced chapters will keep turning the pages of this novel until the end. Well-developed cast of realistic characters that you will relate to one will keep you engaged. One of my favorite things about Moran's books is his entire cast of characters detailed in the back of the book. I admit to reading about the cast first in order to firmly get everyone in my mind. As a follower of his, I know each character is important to the plot and I don't want to miss anything or overlook anyone." – Cold Coffee Cafe

The President is Missing – **Book Three of** *The Matt Blake Mysteries*
http://amzn.to/2t9v7wu

While he was addressing the nation from a submerged nuclear submarine, President Blake's message is suddenly cut off. Anyone listening heard an explosion. The explosion was followed by floating debris five minutes later.

First Lady Dee Blake has doubts, which she shares with naval high command and the new president. She thinks the explosion and the debris were a ruse to make people think the sub was destroyed, and her husband with it.

Could the sub have been hijacked and the president kidnapped? But who would commit such an act? What is its purpose? Was it Russia, China, Iran, or a shadowy group of freelance terrorists?

The new president appoints Dee as his Chief of Staff, with explicit instructions to find the missing submarine—and President Matt Blake.

Her life, and the life of the nation, suddenly take a horrifying turn.

"Russ Moran wrote a true thriller, with a strong plot and even stronger characters. To think that there are good guys—Russian Naval Admirals, no less—made this book not only a solid who-done-it but also a strong 'why did they do it?' " – Unka Heshie

A Climate of Doubt – **Book Four of** *The Matt Blake Mysteries*
https://amzn.to/2OSwcHR

Forget what you ever heard about climate change. Forget your preconceived notions about reality itself. Instantly, you are in a new world, a horrifying world, a world you don't understand.

On a hot summer day, Homeland Security Secretary, Rick Bellamy, and his wife Ellen, a famous TV talk show host, walked along the ocean front trying to escape the heat. Suddenly the temperature dropped from the high 90s to below freezing in a matter of minutes. It began to snow — *on July 16*. The temperatures across the country and the world plummeted, creating winter in summer.

Bellamy and the rest of the government struggled to cope with the suddenly new climate, but to cope, they first had to find out what happened.

Scientists from academia blamed the weather on a sudden acceleration of climate change, but they were unable to explain a 60-degree temperature drop in a matter of minutes. Two astronauts in an American space station realized that the sudden weather calamity coincided with a test of the 20 satellites that the space station controlled. Attention focused on a huge American corporation that owned the space station and the satellites. Could there be a connection between the satellite tests and the radical drop in temperature?

As the deaths piled up and the world economy tilted toward disaster because of gigantic summer blizzards, Rick Bellamy and his team struggled to find answers before it was too late. Was it a sudden shift in climate change or did it have something to do with the satellites? The biggest question remained — was the catastrophe an accident, or was somebody controlling the weather? Was it terror?

"Mr. Moran does a masterful job of crafting an action-packed, suspenseful read about the devastating consequences of climate manipulation. The diabolical mastermind behind the caper is a dictator of the worst kind — a man without conscience who cares only for power. Through the magic of Mr. Moran's digital pen, the men and woman in white hats are three-dimensional and vividly real. While this is a work of fiction, it's plausible fiction. We can easily relate to the horrific consequences of such an act of terrorism as so capably portrayed in Mr. Moran's prose." – Colorado Avid Reader

THE HARRY AND MEG SERIES

The Maltese Incident – A Story of Time Travel – **Book One of** *The Harry and Meg Series*, **the prequel to** *The Violent Sea* **https://amzn.to/2RclZCT**

You're on a beautiful cruise ship. The April sky is full of stars.

Suddenly, the ship rumbles, and instantly the stars disappear.

"What the hell was that?" Captain Fenton yelled. "Beats me, captain. I've never seen anything like it," the first officer said. They would soon discover that the ship, *The Maltese*, had just traveled through time—millions of years to the past.

Captain Harry Fenton, a highly decorated naval war hero, realizes the greatest battle of his life lay ahead of him. Captain Harry, a widow, falls in love with a beautiful passenger, Meg Johnson, an executive with the company that owns the ship.

After a whirlwind romance, they marry—in the ship's ballroom—100 million years in the past. Captain Harry convinces the passengers and crew that they must move ashore to a tropical island because the ship is running out of fuel and supplies. He organizes a group to go ashore and inspect the island.

An ancient forest inhabited by dinosaurs awaits them.

Meg wants to go with them. Harry, fearing for her safety, tries to convince her to stay on the ship. Meg demonstrates that she is proficient with a gun by taking apart a rifle and reassembling it—in 15 seconds. Harry marvels that he's never seen such an expert gun handler—or accurate shooter. So, AR-15 in hand, Meg joins the inspection party. Charging dinosaurs are no match for Meg Fenton's firepower.

Will the 1,000 souls ever make it back to the time they came from, or will they remain stranded in the distant past?

A scientist aboard theorizes that, to return to their present time, they need to go back to the time portal, or wormhole, that brought them to the past. But the ship doesn't have enough fuel for the journey. Realizing that their lives have hit the reset button, the crew and passengers construct a community in the forest—Malta Town.

Under Harry and Meg's leadership, they create a court system, a legislature, and all the elements of a small budding democracy. Meg figures out a way to harness hydroelectric power from a nearby waterfall. Everybody thinks of Harry and Meg as the heart and soul of Malta Town. They begin their new lives—among the dinosaurs.

The Maltese Incident is a riveting tale of time travel, love, courage, and horror.

"As with Moran's work, he continues to be a great storyteller. I recommend reading this from title to end. It's well written, and filled with intensity and levity." – Amy's Bookshelf

The Violent Sea – A Story of Time Travel – Book Two of *The Harry and Meg Series,* the sequel to *The Maltese Incident* https://amzn.to/2AT5ypI

The Violent Sea is a novel of war, time travel, military history. It's the second book in the Harry and Meg Series. It's also a sweet romance between Harry and his wife, Meg.

Rear Admiral Harry Fenton has done it again. He's traveled through time to a different era. He finds himself, with a serious head injury from a fall, at Pearl Harbor Base Hospital on May 16, 1942, three weeks before the Battle of Midway. His wife and aide, Lieutenant Meg Fenton, is worried sick, and waits for him—in 2018.

Admiral Harry is the commanding officer of Carrier Strike Group 14 in 2018, but the people in 1942 think he's a busted-up hallucinating sailor who imagines himself an admiral.

Admiral Raymond Spruance is commanding officer of Carrier Task Force 16. After hearing about Harry's time travel stories, Spruance orders him brought to his flagship, the *USS Enterprise*. After Harry tells him about his time travel experiences, Spruance is convinced the man is insane. But after speaking to him at length, Spruance is amazed at Harry's knowledge of naval tactics and strategy. He calls Harry's bluff and orders him to stay aboard the *Enterprise* for her upcoming engagement at the Battle of Midway. By the end of the battle, Spruance is convinced Harry is an admiral, and thinks of him as a friend.

Now Harry needs to figure out how to travel back to 2018, to his carrier command, but most importantly, to the love of his life, Lieutenant Meg. After Harry returns to the present, the Fentons are deployed on Harry's flagship, the *USS Gerald R. Ford*. The ship encounters another wormhole, this one in the ocean. They are transported to 1944 and participate in the Battle of Leyte Gulf.

The book took me 10 months to write. It went through 20 drafts and three rounds with my editors. I did copious research for the book to ensure its historical accuracy. If you enjoy the genre of time travel, I think you will love this book. I got to know my two main characters in the prequel, The Maltese Incident. Harry and Meg are deeply in love but enjoy constant banter and wisecracks. One of my favorite characters, Admiral Ashley Patterson of The Gray Ship, makes an important cameo appearance in The Violent Sea. – RFM

"What a great book. You will love this book. Time travel telling at its best. At the end you will believe it is possible. Russell Moran has crafted a great continuation from The Maltese Incident his character development has continued from the first book throughout this book and possibly beyond. His writing is so detail oriented you will find yourself believing that time travel is not only real but possible. This

book was given to me as a gift but it turned out to be one of the greatest gifts I have ever received. You will find that your investment of money and time reading this book to be a great investment. Time and money both well spent." – Mike the Mailman

A Sea of Fear – A Novel of Time Travel – **Book Three of** *The Harry and Meg Series*
https://amzn.to/2GERuSx

You're Five-Star Admiral Harry Fenton, whom President Blake calls the greatest fighting admiral in American history.

Along with your Navy Commander wife, Meg, you lead your carrier strike group against the worst enemy the country has faced since World War II, a small nation that is intent on destroying the world's shipping industry. The seas of the world have become scenes of plunder, pillage, and mass murder.

The President has convinced you to come out of retirement and put an end to the looming crisis. He promotes you to Fleet Admiral, the highest-ranking officer since Admiral William Halsey. You and Meg were having a pleasant retirement, running a world-class resort that you bought in Rhode Island. But when the president pleads you to "Give 'em Hell, Harry," you know that you can't ignore his call to duty.

As people who have time traveled in the past, you come up with an idea to travel three years into the future. With President Blake's blessing, you and Meg lead a group of officers into the future. What you find is horrifying, an America taken over by a totalitarian dictator. You return to the past and report your findings. President Blake, hearing your terrifying story, convinces you that you have an even bigger call to duty, the greatest challenge of your life. You take on the challenge for one reason— Meg will be at your side.

As in the first two books of the Harry and Meg Series, *The Maltese Incident* and *The Violent Sea, A Sea of Fear* is a sweet romance between two of literature's most exciting and likable characters, Harry and Meg Fenton. *A Sea of Fear* is a story of war, politics, time travel, and love.

"This story is incredible. I felt like it was real-life and happening NOW! The way the political world is unfolding with the lies and innuendos, something like this could be possible. The main couple, husband and wife, Meg and Harry worked together to solve and help the nation climb onto its rock-solid feet. Surely this is the integrity that the United States government stands for. They had me in their corner wanting to see them win against the evil Antonio Martin. Read the story, it will enthrall and pull you in as it did me...Great ending." – Cristella

The Pineaire Incident – **Book Four of** *The Harry and Meg Series*
https://amzn.to/2VXQ2lp

One hundred gigantic fast submarines suddenly appear in the ocean. President Harry Fenton and his First Lady, Meg are shocked by the event, as are all the leaders of the world. Where are the submarines from? What do they want? What are their intentions?

Six Russian submarines attack one of the mystery subs. All six Russian subs are destroyed in two minutes.

President Fenton, along with Meg, reaches out to contact the leader of the strange fleet. They are amazed to discover that the subs are from another planet, Planet Pineaire. But they're pleased to find out that the Pinearians came in peace, and bring with them an amazing gift, a new type of fuel that can revolutionize life on earth.

Get ready for an interplanetary thrill ride.

"Right at the beginning, we learn that 100 giant submarines are discovered with no idea how they could all suddenly appear. Being familiar with Harry and Meg, I immediately presumed they must have Time Traveled from some future time. Uh Oh, I almost gave away an important detail. You should already know that Harry and Meg are President and First Lady having recently defeated a small rogue nation that destroyed the Cruise Ship industry and nearly took over the world's Shipping Industry. You might think peaceful times are ahead when abruptly, 100 of these 1,800 foot long submarines appear. Five Stars." – The Holey One

THE DETECTIVING SERIES
Until You Came Along - **Book One of** *The Detectiving Series*
https://amzn.to/2MI6TEo

Veteran police detectives Bobbie Nelson and Bob Lawton are partnered. They're both concerned that they may not get along. They're both highly skilled and love their work — They love to solve puzzles. They love *Detectiving*. They soon learn that they don't just love their jobs, they love each other. *Detectiving* is an action-packed police thriller wrapped around a sweet romance.

Bobbie and Bob, the BBs, are two of the most exciting and likeable characters you will find in literature.

"This book should be kept out of the hands of crooks, criminals, terrorists, and any others planning to do evil. There are so many techniques utilized by skilled detectives that are revealed that this book could be used as a training guide by the Bad Guys. Even so, the reality is that fundamental police work is what solves most crimes. Gathering and evaluating massive amounts of data and looking for patterns or repeating details is what our two main characters excel at." – The Holey One

"Russell Moran has done it again with "Detectiving." Each

case builds upon earlier ones, with the BBs fine-tuning their puzzle-solving techniques to such a degree, it's not long before the FBI and CIA reach out them to piece together more complicated scenarios impacting on society. Russell has created an easy-to-read and fast-paced story, which will keep you turning the pages late into the evening to find out what happens next. I can't wait for the next book in the series!" – R. J. Krzak

The Streets of Terror - **Book Two of** *The Detectiving Series* https://amzn.to/3bmiqEh

The further adventures of Bobbie Nelson and Bob Lawton, now married. NYPD Detectives First Grade Bobbie Nelson and Bob Layton are partners, husband and wife, and, as Bobbie loves to say, best friends. They both agree that the day they were partnered was the luckiest day of their lives. Police Commissioner Ralph Norquist is their boss and also their good friend. He nicknames them, "the BBs." Norquist discovers that he can assign the most difficult cases to them and they will get the job done. It's almost routine the way they solve child kidnapping cases, serial killer murders, attacks on subway trains, a huge case of drone attacks on football stadiums, and Internet fraud attacks on senior citizens. But what never becomes routine is their love for each other. When they get to their office in the morning, they begin the day with a hug and a kiss. Their partnership almost ended when Bobbie was shot in the head at a crime scene.

She spent six long weeks in a semi-comatose state. Bob said it was the worst six weeks of his life, not knowing if Bobbie would fully recover. Fortunately, the bullet wound did no permanent brain damage, and Bobbie came back to her old self, including her photographic memory. Besides being famous detectives, they're also talented writers. Bob had written a best-selling crime novel before they met, and they both collaborated on a nonfiction book on the art of being a detective - *Detectiving*. That book became a runaway best seller and the royalties poured in. Their book profits, combined with a generous inheritance from Bob's uncle, as well as their combined salaries, made them more than comfortable financially. They renovated their apartment near police headquarters. Bob had bought the building before they met.

After a neighboring tenant moved out. They knocked down a wall and created a 3,000 square foot apartment, a three-block walk from One Police Plaza. Realizing that they need to get away from their hectic work occasionally, they bought a beautiful mansion in East Hampton, and they love to spend weekends there with friends and family—until they discover they are being stalked by a serial killer.

Together We Win - **Book Three of** *The Detectiving Series*

Detectives First Grade with the NYPD, Bobbie Nelson and Bob Lawton are husband and wife, professional partners, and lovers. Bobbie often says that they're also best friends. Bobbie was hired away from the Chicago Police Department and they were partnered, causing Bobbie to say, "I'm the luckiest cop in the world."

Bobbie is shot and seriously wounded with a non-life-threatening brain injury, the most trying event either them had ever faced. She fully recovers and she and Bob continue their work as the greatest detectives in the country. Their friend and boss, NYPD Commissioner Ralph Norquist, nicknamed them the BBs. *The New York Times* dubs them "New York's Dynamic Detective Duo."

They embark on some of the toughest assignments in the NYPD, including bombings of NYC subway trains, terrorist drone attacks on football stadiums, a fraud ring that zeroes on elderly people's bank accounts, a child kidnapping plot, and a serial killer who specialized in murdering young couples.

Commissioner Norquist never hesitates to assign the most

difficult cases in the department to the BBs. He even refers to them as *NYPD Royalty*.

The Long Island Project – Book Four of The Detectiving Series
https://amzn.to/2WgJC2n

"Another winner!"

Our old friends, Detectives Bobbie Nelson and Bob Lawton, "the BBs," are engaged in the most frightening case of their career, an armed quarantine of Long Island by a sinister group. To find the answer to the problem, they travel through time to 1942, and discover the problem is larger than they had thought.

The third novel in Russell's Patterns Series, we meet up again with the infamous detectives, Bobbie Nelson and Bob Lawson as they're called upon to solve another problem. Why is Long Island under quarantine, and who is behind it? Before long, they uncover a conspiracy, which could lead a takeover through mind control and time travel.

"As with all of Moran's novels, the characters adapt to the situations they find themselves in and their interactions bring the best out in the 'good guys and gals' and will turn readers against those behind the conspiracy. There's plenty of intrigue for everyone as the 'BBs' solve their latest puzzle. I look forward to their next adventure!" – RK

Robot Depot
http://amzn.to/2zXW7C2

Mike Bateman is a visionary businessman, the creator and CEO of the fabulously successful chain of stores, Robot Depot, a company dedicated to selling robots and Artificial Intelligence machines for a variety of uses.

The company is a darling of Wall Street and is the most popular destination for consumers and businesses looking for labor saving devices. But the company caught the eye of ISIS, the terrorist Islamic State. They discover a great way to deliver bombs – using the products of Robot Depot to kill people. Robot Depot changed from being a popular company to an object of fear because of the tampered products it sells. The terrorists use the company for "terror spectaculars," including the destruction of a skyscraper, a drone attack on Yankee Stadium, and the bombing of a children's sailing regatta.

Mike Bateman and the FBI are in a race to stop his products from becoming weapons, a race to stop the wanton killings. His wife and partner, Jenny, discovers the true meaning of terror one horrible summer day.

"Moran just got a new fan. This is the first book of Moran's that I've read, but I look forward to reading more of his work. I enjoyed this story, and found that Moran is not only a good writer, but he's a good storyteller as well. It's an interesting and creative story, mixing new technology and AI uses, with terrorism. It's a thriller that keeps the reader turning the page, and it's extremely captivating. I enjoyed the story and look forward to future works of his." – Amy's Bookshelf

Leonardo Murphy – A Coming of Age Thriller
https://amzn.to/31vzC4S

You just launched a satellite into space without a rocket. You invented a computer algorithm that writes novels. You just entered Harvard University on a full scholarship after completing high school in two years. Not bad for a 12-year-old kid.

Leonardo changed his name from William to Leonardo to honor his hero, Leonardo da Vinci. Young Leonardo Murphy has the second highest IQ ever recorded. Now 25, he met a beautiful young woman named Janice, and fell madly in love. They married a year later.

Janice and Leonardo, whom she calls "Lee," collaborate on various projects with the CIA and FBI. But their intelligence activities put a target on their backs. They narrowly escape four assassination attempts.

Leonardo Murphy is a breathtakingly fast coming-of-age thriller about one of the most fascinating characters you will ever meet in literature. Instantly, you are shoulder to shoulder with the world's most amazing genius.

"Finally, a believable super hero comes to life! Peaks and valleys of horrific actions are neatly juxtaposed against comic relief. The humor, ranging between the poles of mild to downright hysterical, will surely tickle your funny bone. The frequent use of the protagonist's favorite word (26 matches found throughout), which I won't divulge, would ordinarily belabor one's prose, save when Leonardo employs the term. As a matter of fact, the story concludes with that very word, but rather endearingly. No, I did not ruin the ending for you folks. You'll see." – Robert Banfelder

The Silent Author
https://amzn.to/3cBLRlR

Author Melanie Pierce is widely acknowledged to be the country's greatest novelist. Suddenly she faces the worst form of censorship imaginable – *Editorial Terrorism*. Her words are no longer her own. Before she can publish a book, she, and her fellow authors, must submit the manuscript to a shadowy group of terrorists. Failure to do so will result in the death of one of her loved ones.

A page-turning thriller about a famous page-turning author. Melanie's husband, Max Wakefield, is an FBI agent, and has been assigned to lead what had become known as *The Silent Author Case*. His dedication as an FBI agent, as well as his deep love for his wife, Melanie, launched Max into the most dangerous assignment of his career.

"A thrilling plot shifting page turner about a page turning author." – LK

A Charter Through Time
https://amzn.to/34f9BM4

Former federal prosecutor, Janey Drake, has resigned her legal job because she could no longer put up with the stress of prosecuting drug dealers and the frustrating meanderings of the criminal justice system. She decides to resign after an ironclad case was dismissed by a "caring" judge. She takes on a new life that she loves, chartering her 60-foot yacht that was a gift from her wealthy father. An experienced large boat captain, Janey has found a cure for the high stress work of her former occupation. She also found a cure for her loneliness when she met the man of her dreams by a chance encounter in a diner. Jack Fleming is a famous novelist and loves his work, and soon finds out that he loves Janey, his accidental friend from the diner. He and Janey fall impossibly in love with each other and found a way to blend their lives—cruising the high seas and writing about it. Janey has taken on the role as Jack's editor and she couldn't be happier.

But suddenly their happy lives together take on a frightening new dimension. While cruising off New London, Connecticut, their boat encounters a wormhole or time portal, and they find themselves two years into the future, a horrifying future that had seen a nuclear war. They find out that their apartment building in Manhattan was the target for one of the bombs. Yes, they discover that they had been killed, two years ago. But yet they're alive. Time travel is a strange phenomenon, and sometimes a scary one.

They realize that they have no choice. They must return to the past and warn the government about the coming horror.

They begin the most terrifying experience of their lives—how to go back in time and prevent your own death, and the deaths of millions of others.

"A time-travel mind bender." – LK

The Love We Almost Lost
https://amzn.to/2G8iMnR

Regulations frown upon a military doctor being romantically involved with a patient.

But Lieutenant Rebecca Lang, a Navy physician, frowned upon the regulations. She fell madly in love with Captain Jack Parker, a wounded Marine officer under her care at Bagram Airbase in Afghanistan.

Doctor Rebecca, or Becca as she prefers to be called, felt that she had a rare bond with Captain Jack. It began as a simple doctor-patient relationship, then developed into a friendship, then, after constant flirting, it became a serious love affair. Captain Jack was happy that Becca ignored the regulations, and so was she.

When they were discharged from the military within two weeks of each other, they looked forward to making their relationship permanent, and planned to marry. But, on the day Jack returned to the States, he was mugged, and suffered a multi-year mental blackout from amnesia. Becca didn't know where he was, and she assumed he was dead after such a long absence. Becca sees Jack interviewed on TV, although the man doesn't think he's Jack because he suffers from severe amnesia. When they meet, Jack comes out of his amnesia and his mind remembers the woman his heart had never forgotten. They resume their love and their lives together. Becca, widely recognized as the nation's expert on infectious diseases, is tapped by the White House to combat a deadly virus that has been set loose on the world.

Jack, who by now has become an FBI Agent, joins his wife Becca in the most terrifying struggle they ever experienced — the fight to save humanity.

THE WORMHOLE ADVENTURES
The Wormhole Gang – Book 1 of *The Wormhole Adventures*
https://amzn.to/3nTxLlN

"Jack, where the hell are we?"

Admiral Ashley Patterson, the Navy's youngest admiral at age 39, was with her husband, famous publisher Jack Thurber. Jack is a commander in the Naval Reserve, and often accompanies Ashley on assignments. They were on their most enjoyable deployment to date. Ashley had been given command of the famous *USS Intrepid*, an aircraft carrier that had become a museum, a three-month post that was largely ceremonial. The Navy's thinking was that Ashley's new command would be an excellent way to promote the museum, as well as a great public relations stunt for the Navy. Both history lovers, they were enjoying Ashley's latest assignment — until they came to face with the most horrifying situation they ever encountered.

One early morning they awoke, expecting to see themselves alongside Pier 86. Instead, they were shocked to see that they were in the middle of the ocean. While they slept, the ship, without an engine or other discernible source of power, suddenly left its dock on the West Side of Manhattan—with nobody at the controls. They realized that the ship had gone through a time portal, a wormhole.

They were lost at sea—and lost in time.

Along with two other crew members, they formed a group to discover what had happened to them. Admiral Ashley named the group *The Wormhole Gang*.

"This book takes time travel to a wild new level. I feel like I know the characters personally." – JC Prince.

The Wormhole Crisis – Book 2 of *The Wormhole Adventures*
https://amzn.to/3nTxLlN

Admiral Ashley Patterson and her husband, famous publisher Jack Thurber, have done it again, not that they were planning on it. They crossed a wormhole, a portal in time, a gateway to a different world.

They had done it before, but this one was different—This wormhole was man-made.

President Matt Blake realized that the country was in the grips of a crisis, one which he dubbed *The Wormhole Crisis*.

Recognizing Admiral Patterson's talent for fearless leadership, he promoted her to Fleet Admiral, the highest rank in the Navy. At the same time, he appointed her Chairwoman of the Joint Chiefs of Staff, the highest position in the American military.

The President knew he had a horrifying crisis to solve, and who better to lead the effort than Admiral Patterson. He put her in charge of *Operation Wormhole Kill*, along with her close husband, Jack. Together they embarked on a terrifying attempt to save the world from man-made time travel.

A rogue nation had manufactured a wormhole-creating satellite, one which can inflict a wormhole anywhere on earth. The problem got worse when that nation created an instrument on the satellite that can detonate a bomb on earth — from space.

The only way to deal with a wormhole is to recross it to find your way back to the time you came from. But the rogue nation created a new type of wormhole — one that didn't enable you to recross it.

One horrifying night, the evening of the annual State of the Union Address, saw the ultimate result of the terrifying satellite, one that could spell the end of the world. Instantly the fate of the world changed, especially for Admiral Patterson. It was a new world, a world Ashley could never have imagined.

The fate of mankind was now in Admiral Patterson's hands.

About the Author

In addition to the 26 novels discussed above, I also published five nonfiction books: *Justice in America: How it Works – How it Fails; The APT Principle: The Business Plan That You Carry in Your Head; Boating Basics: The Boattalk Book of Boating Tips; If You're Injured: A Consumer Guide to Personal Injury Law*; *How to Create More Time*. My latest nonfiction book is *The Novel – A Writer's Guide – Discover the Joy of Writing Fiction*. I'm a lawyer and a veteran of the United States Navy. I live on Long Island, New York, with my wife and editor, Lynda, and a Golden Retriever named Maggie. Maggie makes a cameo appearance in many of my books.

A Personal Request

I hope you enjoyed reading *The Streets of Terror* as much as I enjoyed writing it.

Please consider leaving a brief review on amazon.com. It doesn't need to be lengthy or elaborate, just your thoughts on the characters, the scenes, and the story. Book reviews are the lifeblood of an author.

I deeply thank you.

Russ Moran